Willa by Heart

Willa by Heart

Coleen Murtagh Paratore

SCHOLASTIC INC.
New York Toronto London Auckland Sydney
Mexico City New Delhi Hong Kong Buenos Aires

ISBN-13: 978-0-545-10434-0
ISBN-10: 0-545-10434-3

12 11 10 9 8 7 6 5 4 3 2 1   9 10 11 12 13 14/0

Printed in the U.S.A.   40

First Scholastic printing, January 2009

Book design by Daniel Roode
The text for this book is set in Berkeley.

To my beautiful sister,
Noreen Mahoney,
with my deepest admiration.
I love you, Neen.
—Col

Contents

When life throws you a pit, plant a cherry tree.

—Willa Havisham

CHAPTER 1

Lucky Days

We'll begin at dawn.

—Thornton Wilder, *Our Town*

When I see the sun rise out of the sea, sometimes I think I will burst with thanks for a world so lovely as this. There is such hope in that moment, such possibility.

Before the sun comes, I sit alone on the cliff, staring at the rainbow ribbons out where the water meets the sky, and I wait with the wind and waves, the gulls and fish, the morning star, even the moon sometimes, we're all together waiting, waiting, until, at some silent moment, the horizon hatches before our eyes and a diamond bird of light bursts upward, wet and shining from its sea-mother nest.

Promise me you will watch the sunrise at least once in your life.

It is a miracle. God grand.

If I miss the sunrise but I am still the first to arrive on the beach, those are lucky days too. I sink my foot in the sand like a flag, an explorer claiming new land. I survey the scene before me and smile. Mine, all mine.

This morning I walk out onto the Spit, a narrow peninsula about a mile long, the Atlantic all around. Bay on one side, ocean on the other. I know this place by heart.

Today I start on the bay path, the calmer, peaceful side. The wind blows soft against my cheeks, the waves lap gentle as a lamb. On the other side, on some days, the surf soars and wind roars mighty as a lion. And all that separates the lamb and the lion is this little strip of land.

Just sand, really. Grains of sand. Millions and millions of them.

Alone, each is barely visible. Together they make a beach.

Once upon a time the Spit was so big there were hotels along it. Hurricanes and nor'easters have taken their toll. So has the pounding of countless feet, beachcombers like me. Each year the Spit gets skinnier. It could wash away any time now. One good storm might do it. It's important that its backbone, the sand dune, stays strong.

The sand dune runs spinelike down the center of the Spit. When I was little, the dune was a mountain, thrilling and forbidden. Up, up, up I would plod, stand panting victoriously proud on top, then run slip-slide-giggling down.

Now the mountain is a hill. I can see across it in spots.

Frosting the dune is a field of sea grass, long, flowing green hair. Small birds, gray-and-white plovers and terns, for some reason choose to nest here. Then, once they do, those silly little birds imagine they are bigger than they are. They fight bravely to fend off heavy-pawed dragon-dogs running free from their owners' leashes and the aerial assaults of seagull monsters searching for breakfast eggs.

Yesterday was warm for April. It is cooler this morning. Feathers of fog flit past me like fairies. I swipe them away and laugh.

When I was little and first came to Cape Cod, summers to visit Nana, fog used to scare me. Fog wasn't weather at all. Fog was a ghost that would swallow me up if I didn't hurry home and hide. Now fog seems ethereal, romantic.

I reach for the silver heart, the locket Joseph Frances Kennelly, JFK, gave me on Valentine's Day. He looked so handsome that night, brown hair skimming the collar of his tuxedo, blue eyes glittering in the firelight. I thought I might faint. I kept telling myself, *Breathe, Willa, breathe.*

He knew I was disappointed when I opened the locket and it was empty. Two halves of a heart, no pictures. The dimple on his cheek deepened as he smiled. "The *girl* decides who to put in it. But . . . I hope you decide it's me."

"Oh, it's you," I said, and I kissed him. I kissed him first. Then we danced in the barn, just the two of us, the most perfect night of my life.

When I reach the tip of the Spit and turn, I can almost feel the ocean current shift. I am on the lion side now. Wind fills my ears and whips my hair back. I close my eyes and breathe it in. Everything seems more alive here. Louder, faster, saltier. Two seagulls are trying to out-squawk each other, battling for the same poor scuttling crab. No fishermen this morning, not a single boat. Maybe a storm was forecast.

On clear days as I walk, I look for beach glass and orange-and-yellow jingle shells. Sometimes I find buoys, lures, castle pails. Last week an emerald earring, just one.

The fog is getting thicker now. It wets my face like rain. I pick up my pace. I'm late anyway. I'm on breakfast duty at the inn.

My family owns the Bramblebriar Inn, just outside the center of town. I hope Rosie is making blueberry pancakes, warm maple syrup, sausage on the side . . . *wait* . . . there's something ahead there on the jetty, out on the final rock. I walk forward, the fog growing thicker. It's hard to see anything clearly.

As I get closer, I can see it's not a fisherman, no pole. How odd to be just standing there out on the edge of a jetty on a morning like this. How curious.

I walk closer. The figure turns. It is a girl, about my age. She looks familiar, but I'm not sure. "Hi," I shout over the wind. The girl stares at me. She cranes her head forward, side to side, looking, as if she, too, is trying to see if she knows me.

I reach the jetty and nearly slip as I step up onto the first boulder. The fog is thickening like pudding. The girl is motioning to come closer, or maybe just waving. I guess we do know each other. "Hi," I say again, louder. I hop over to the next boulder, then the next, careful not to slip. Wouldn't want to fall in on a day like this, not able to spot jagged rocks and coral, not to mention the eels. I hop across to another flat spot.

Just then there's a break in the fog. I can see her face. Dark eyes and skin, long curly black hair. She is beautiful. The girl smiles as if we know each other. I have never seen her before. The wind is picking up, waves crashing in louder, must be nearly high tide. These last several boulders will be covered with water soon. It won't be safe to stand. "Hi," I say again.

The girl nods and then turns back toward the sea. She spreads her arms wide like a heron before flight, then raises them above her gracefully and dives.

What? It's too early in the season to swim. Even for the bravest, Cape water won't be warm for months. I leap onto the next rock, then the next, and when I reach the last, I look down. I don't see her anywhere.

I stand there looking, looking. She has to come up for air. I call to the foaming water, "Hey! Are you all right?" Did she swim left or right or straight out? I search and search. It starts to rain.

Shivering, I zip my jacket, pull up the hood. I keep scanning the water. "Hello. Are you okay?" Where is she? Why hasn't she surfaced? My heart is pounding. What if she hurt herself? What if she . . .

I head back fast along the slippery rocks, and when I reach the beach, I start running, eyes glued to the water as I go. Where did she go? Why doesn't she come up for air? I'm definitely late now. Mother will be mad. I run toward the beach stairs. My bike is at the top. I'll phone for help at the nearest cottage. As I run, I stare, eyes burning, fixed on the water, searching, searching. Where is she?

And then all of a sudden, the girl's head pops up. She looks toward the shore like a carefree harbor seal. I run to the edge of the water and scream, "Are you okay?"

"Yes," she shouts, treading water, wiping hair away from her eyes.

"Are you *sure* you're okay?" I ask.

"Yes," the girl shouts, sounding annoyed. *"Are you?"*

CHAPTER 2

Talk About Surprises

Anything serious goin' on in the world since Wednesday?

—*Our Town*

Am I okay? Am I okay? Unbelievable. I'm fuming as I bike home, cold in the rain. Here I was worried about *her*, trying to help *her*, and she acted mad at *me!* Who was that girl, anyway? And she was on my beach, *my beach.*

It isn't until I turn the corner on to my street, see the old stone fence and the Bramble Board message, SPRING FORWARD TOWARD YOUR DREAMS, that I feel myself calming down. A girl couldn't ask for a nicer home than the Bramblebriar Inn.

Happy yellow daffodils, cheery pink and purple

tulips, line the winding driveway. I park my bike, head up the porch stairs. Mmmmm, breakfast smells delicious.

When my mother married Sam Gracemore last year, we renovated his grandmother's old estate and opened the Bramblebriar Inn. People in town said we'd uncovered a treasure. Mom gave up her wedding-planning business and Sam gave up teaching to run the place. I help in the kitchen and take care of the library, the game room, and the Bramble Board.

The Bramblebriar Inn is elegant, but warm and cozy, too. When our guests come back to visit us, again and again, we welcome them home like family.

The main house is three stories high, white with green shutters, four tall brick chimneys, and a widow's walk on the back rooftop. On a clear day you can see Nantucket Sound. There are thirty rooms in the main house and several smaller buildings on the property; a renovated barn big enough for dances and parties; acres of grass, trees, and flowers; a huge, round garden labyrinth; and a pond where you can swim in the summer and ice-skate in the winter.

"Sorry I'm late, Rosie. Be right there." I flip my wet sandals off by the door and race up to change. My stepfather, Sam, is the main chef at the inn, but we just hired Rosie to handle breakfast and desserts. My freshman English teacher, Dr. Swaminathan, went to India on family business, and Sam is substituting for him this semester. I'll miss Dr. Swammy, but I'm happy to have Sam back as my teacher again. That's how I first met Sam. He was my seventh-grade English teacher. From the moment I met Sam, I knew he would be the perfect husband for my mother, the perfect father for me. I spent months playing Cupid, trying to get them together, and finally it worked.

I still call Sam, Sam, but I am planning on calling him Dad on Father's Day. I think that's the best gift I could give him. It's been a long time since anyone called Sam Dad. Sam was married before, long ago, but his wife and son were killed in a car crash. His little boy was only two.

When I come down to the kitchen, Rosie is dicing vegetables with the flair of a celebrity chef on television. She puts me to work squeezing oranges for juice.

Rosie can't be more than twenty. She has a baby

named Liliana. Nana told me that Rosie's husband ran off after the baby was born and never came back. Nana heard about the situation and helped Rosie get the job here.

I think it must be so sad for Rosie, having her husband abandon her like that, and so hard having to leave her baby to come here, but Rosie doesn't bring her troubles to work. She's friendly to me, Mom, and Sam, but she keeps her private life private.

"How was your walk, Willa?" Rosie asks.

"Okay," I say. I'll wait and tell my friend Tina about that annoying girl in the water. "What are you making, Rosie? It smells wonderful."

"Frittatas, home fries, cranberry nut muffins."

"Mmmm, can't wait."

"Morning, ladies," Sam says, coming into the kitchen. "Willa, your mom said another magazine called yesterday. You won't let all this fame go to your head, will you?" Sam winks at me and smiles.

"No way, Sam." I guess I should tell you I'm something of a celebrity here in Bramble. People say I saved the Bramble Library, which I guess is true. Last September I was elected head of Community Service for the freshman class at

Bramble Academy, and we had to find a way to make a difference. My friend Sulamina Mum, she's a minister, said to pick a cause I cared about. Well, I heard that the Bramble Library was being shut down. They were going to send all of our books, *Bramble books*, over to the Falmouth Library. I was so mad I couldn't see straight. That's another thing you should know about me. I love books. I mean I love, love, love, love, *love* books. And that was my library, *my library*. No way would I let them close it.

The freshman class put on dance parties here in the barn and then a fancy Valentine's prom to raise money, but it still wasn't enough. It looked like the library was lost, until lo and behold, our favorite inn guests, the Blazers, of the Blazer Buick fortune, came through with the big bucks, and long story short, the Bramble Library lives.

Mom comes in freshly showered after her morning run. She grabs a bottle of water from the fridge, then whispers something to Sam, and he says, "Sure, Stella, okay."

"Willa," Mom says, "can we talk to you for a minute?"

Rosie looks uncomfortable, like maybe she

should leave, but she can't. The guests will be expecting breakfast at eight.

"Why don't we go into the library," Sam says.

This sounds serious. Oh no, what now? Is everything all right with Nana? Is everything all right with the inn? They aren't thinking of selling it, are they?

Mom and Sam sit next to each other on the couch. He wraps his arm around her and says something I can't hear.

"We have some news," Mom says. "I know this may come as a bit of a surprise to you, Willa . . . but Sam and I . . . are going to have a baby."

What? My stomach somersaults.

Mom smiles at Sam. He nods at her. The tide is changing in my brain.

Sam looks at me, tilts his head to the side, squinting his eyes like he's trying to read my thoughts, like he's wondering if I'm okay with this.

Talk about surprises. It was always just me and Mom. Now me, Mom, and Sam. I've been an only child for fourteen years. I'm a freshman in high school, for gosh sakes . . . *And now I'm going to get a little brother or . . .*

"Willa," Mom says, walking toward me, "are you okay?"

I burst into tears. I hug her. "I'm so happy for you, Mom. And Sam."

When I hug Sam, he keeps his hands locked on my shoulders and stares into my eyes like he's trying to read them. Sam knows that "happy" isn't the only feeling I'm feeling right now. "Willa . . . ," Sam starts, but I shake my head no. I don't want to spoil my mother's joy. "I'm good, Sam. I'm late for Tina's."

Now I really need to talk to my best friend.

CHAPTER 3

Maybe She's a Mermaid

*I've got to tell you something, because if I don't . . .
I'll burst.*

—*Our Town*

When I get to the Belles' house, Tina is up in her room sprawled out on her bed, studying the new Hotties catalog.

"Hey, Willa, perfect timing. Which bikini do you like better, this one or this one?"

I look at the bathing suits. "They're pretty. Why don't you get both?"

"Oh good, Willa, thanks, you're right." Tina breathes a sigh of relief. "I was feeling a little guilty because I already ordered three yesterday and I'm reaching my card max for the month, and Daddy's threatening to cut me off again, but hey, you can never have too many bikinis, right?"

"Right," I say, sticking my chest forward, picturing the boring navy blue one-piece in my drawer from last year. I look at the models in the Hotties catalog. It would take a miracle between now and beach season for me to look like a hottie in one of those bikinis. Maybe I should do more push-ups, eat more broccoli or something.

"Here, Willa." Tina hands me the catalog. "Take it. We get a bunch of these a month—Mom and I are Gold Club customers. Maybe you'll see something you like. And don't be afraid to show off your shape. You have such a cute little shape."

The word "cute" grates on my ears. I'm sick of being cute. Nobody calls Tina cute. People call Tina gorgeous. She has a face like a movie star's and long, silky blond white hair, like the angel wig I wore in the kindergarten Christmas pageant.

"Tina, wait till you hear this. I have really big news. Mom and Sam are expecting a baby."

"A little sister?" Tina claps her hands, all excited. "Ooooooooh, how *cute*!" She bops up and down on the bed. "A little sister? Oooh, I can't wait. Tell Stella I'll babysit anytime, all the time, for free. Oh,

Willa, we'll have such fun shopping for her, dressing her up, taking her out to lunch. . . ." Tina leans forward, her big brown eyes sparkling, "Just think about all those tiny baby dresses, shoes, pocketbooks . . . oh my gosh, we've got to get her tiny baby ears pierced . . . and take her to the spa for her first little mani-pedi . . . in pink, of course—"

"Whoa, Tina, wait. She's not even born yet. And what if it's a boy?"

"Hmmmmm." Tina's face darkens. "Well, that would rule out the mini mani-pedis. . . ." Then she quickly lights up again. "But baby-boy clothes are fun! Aunt Amber loves buying stuff for her nephew. Little farmer jeans and baseball caps . . ." Tina stands up. "Anyway, I'm not worried," she says, flipping her hair back, case closed. "I know it will be a girl."

Tina looks at me. "But what about the big sister? Are you okay with this?"

"Well, it is a big shock. I couldn't believe it at first. I had no idea they wanted a baby. I mean, they're sort of old for it, aren't they? And I'm in high school. I mean, it would have been nice to have somebody to play with when I was little, but . . ."

"Oh, Willa, come on. It will be so much fun."

"I guess you're right. I'm starting to like the idea a bit. . . ."

Tina claps her hands. "Good. Now, can I be her godmother? I want to be the first to know when she's born. Okay? The first."

"Well, I can promise you fourth, maybe. Mom . . . Sam . . . me . . . then you. Deal?"

"Deal."

We get a bowl of chips and some soda. I tell Tina about this morning on the Spit. About the strange girl on the edge of the jetty who dived off into the fog. "And here I thought she drowned. I was all worried, shouting to her, running to call the police, and then all of a sudden she surfaces like a seal and asks if *I'm okay*."

"Wow," Tina says, "and you didn't recognize her?"

"No. At first I thought she looked familiar, but no, I've never seen her before."

"That's weird," Tina says. "Who goes swimming alone that early in the morning? In April? On Cape Cod? Jamaica, maybe, Cancún, maybe, but Cape Cod, no way. That water's freezing. She must be an Eskimo."

"I don't think she's from around here."

"Well, it's way too early for tourists," Tina says, "and it's not a holiday weekend . . . wait, Willa, hold everything." Tina's mouth drops and her eyes go bug wide. "Maybe she's a mermaid."

"Tina." I crack up laughing. "This isn't a movie."

"No, really, she could be."

"Yeah, right. Listen, you mentioned your aunt Amber. How's her business doing?" Tina's aunt Amber owns a matchmaking company called the Perfect Ten. Aunt Amber says the secret to love is finding the person you have ten important things in common with—similar views on religion, politics, having a family. . . .

That gave Tina the idea to make up a compatibility questionnaire for our Valentine's dance. Questions like, what's your favorite ice cream, sport, pizza topping? Tina insisted that everybody had to answer the questions. Normally, the boys would have bolted, but we had a hook. One of them would win a date with my friend Suzanna Jubilee Blazer, the southern-belle beauty-pageant-winning daughter of the Blazer Buick family I mentioned before.

Tina sent the completed questionnaires to Aunt

Amber, who fed the information into her computer. The matching couples were announced at the dance. I never got to go to the dance after all the work of planning it because I broke my foot during a yodeling accident that morning. It's a long story. Anyway, it all turned out perfectly in the end. JFK left the dance early and came to the inn. He threw a stone up at my bedroom window to get my attention.

When I saw him standing there so beautiful in his tux, I nearly fainted. I changed into my pink gown, spritzed on some perfume, and hobbled down the stairs. We danced in the barn, and he gave me the locket. It was the most romantic night of my life. Now we are officially a couple. We talk every day, go out to dinner and the movies. . . .

But as I'm remembering that night he gave me the locket, I start getting angry again. Ruby Sivler has that effect on me. You see, just when JFK gave me the locket, and I was laughing and crying, so happy, he said, "Guess who my match was for that compatible couple thing?" I said, "I don't know, who?" all the while screaming hopefully, *"Me, me,"* inside.

"It was you," JFK said, "and another girl too."

Ruby Sivler. I was sure of it. Ruby's been after Joseph since seventh grade. I just knew she'd find a way to fudge the answers so she'd appear to be his perfect match. I started fuming inside, thinking how I'd get back at Ruby for cheating, when all of a sudden JFK said, "But the eleventh question broke the tie." JFK and I were the real perfect match after all. Of course. And before I knew it, I kissed him. I kissed him. I kissed him *first*. And we slow-danced while cupid fluttered above us up in the rafters. . . .

"Willa?" Tina says. "Earth to Willa."

"Sorry. I was thinking about how Ruby fudged the compatibility test so she could get matched with Joseph at the dance. When is she going to stop being such a sneaky . . ."

Tina has a weird look on her face. The look she gets when she's hiding something. "So," Tina says, picking up the Hotties catalog. "What else should I order?"

"Tina?"

"What?"

"You're hiding something."

"No, I'm not."

— 21 —

"Yes, you are."

"No."

"Yes."

"No."

"Tina, stop it. Tell me. What?"

Tina's face scrunches up like, *Are you sure you want to know?*

My heart is pounding. This can't be good. "Tell me, Tina, what?"

"Okay." Tina sits back down on the bed. "Now, don't start getting all worried, I worry about you worrying so much, but there was this girl at the Valentine's dance—"

"Who? What girl?"

"I don't know," Tina says. "She was wearing this glittery eye mask, you know, like they do at a costume ball, and everybody was wondering who she was. Then Dr. Swammy—oh, he looked handsome in his white tuxedo—"

"Stick to the story, Tina."

"Okay, sorry. So Swammy announced the Compatibly Cupid Dance and started naming the couples. He called out me and Jessie. Oh, I wish you could have seen how hot Jessie looked . . . okay, sorry, and then Swammy called, 'Joseph

Kennelly and Willa Havisham,' and then, "Joseph Kennelly and Mariel . . .' somebody or other.

"Everybody was like, 'Mariel who?' Some guy shouted, 'Way to go, Joe, two for one.' And then the girl with the mask in the green gown edged her way forward and stood right next to Joseph. 'Is that Willa?' Jessie asked me. And I'm like, 'Duh, no, Willa's home with a broken foot.' And then I reminded Dr. Swammy about the tiebreaker, and he said, 'Thank you, Tina,' and he consulted the eleventh question tiebreaker list and announced, 'Joseph Kennelly and Willa Havisham.' And the girl in the mask turned and walked out of the room without saying a word. In fact, I don't think I heard her say a word all night. It was really strange. . . ."

"Tina, why didn't you tell me?" I feel like I'm under water.

"Oh, Willa, you were so happy about the locket and kissing JFK and your private little prom in the barn that I didn't want to spoil it for you. I knew you'd start worrying. You worry way too much, honey, and there's no reason to. Joey Kennelly is obviously crazy about you. . . ."

"Describe her to me, Tina. This Mariel."

"Well, you couldn't really see her face because of the mask. But her skin was dark and beautiful, and she had this amazing black, ringlety hair. . . ."

CHAPTER 4

My Town

Very ordinary town, if you ask me. . . .
But our young people here seem to like it well
enough.

—*Our Town*

My stomach is a tide pool swirling. *Why can't*
anything stay perfect for two seconds? On the way
home from Tina's, I stop at Mum's. I always feel
better when I talk to Mum.

Sulamina Mum is the minister of Bramble
United Community, "a home for every heart." You
don't have to be any certain religion to belong.
Mum says we're all connected back to the very
same one and only god and that the only prayer
we need is two words, "thank you."

I love Mum. She's like another mother to me.
Except she's my friend.

"Hello, Willa," Mum calls, happy to see me. She's sweeping her porch steps. "How's it going?"

"Okay."

Mum stops sweeping and looks at me, hard. She lowers herself down on the top step and pats the spot next to her. "Sit and spill, little sister, sit and spill."

I tell Mum about the masked mystery girl, Mariel, and how she was a perfect match for JFK at the Dream dance and how I have this awful suspicion that she was the girl I saw swimming in the fog this morning and what does that all mean . . . and on top of that, all of a sudden after fourteen years my mother has decided to have a baby and how embarrassing, since I'm a freshman in high school and . . .

Mum listens without saying a word. I love that about Mum. She's the best listener I know. When I finish, she takes a deep breath and lets it out slow. "Hmmmph. I agree. That sure is a lot to hold in your heart."

"Well, what should I do?"

Mum takes another deep breath and lets it out more slowly than the last. "The way I see it, Willa, nothing much you can do, about either situation."

We sit there quiet for a minute. The wind chimes tinkle softly. A bee buzzes by.

"So, what's your new cause going to be?" Mum says.

"My *new* cause?"

"For Community Service. You're still the leader, right?"

"Right."

"And you're done saving the library, right?"

"Right." I see where this conversation is headed.

"And it's only, what, April first, and you've got nearly three months left of school . . . hmmmph . . ." Mum raises her eyebrows, shrugs, and then stares off straight ahead.

I never knew a person who could say so much without saying a single word.

"Okay, okay. I get it." I laugh. "We should find another good cause, another way to make a difference, right?" I stand up and shake my head. "Anybody ever told you you'd make a good spiritual director, Mum, like say a minister or something?"

"Seems to me I've been told that once or twice in my lifetime."

Mum's front door opens, and cane first, foot

second, Riley Truth steps out. Riley is Mum's long-lost high school sweetheart. They just reconnected at Christmas. I sort of played cupid, since I was the one who kept encouraging Mum to try and track him down. And she did. And he came. And they've been happy as honey ever since. I just hope they won't move back down South. I'd be so sad if Mum left Bramble. It would be like the sun leaving the—

"Join us for a walk, Willa?" Riley says. "I promised this pretty lady the first ice cream cone of the season. Although it's sure stone colder up here than home, isn't it, Sully?"

Mum laughs and holds out her hand. Riley helps her up. Mum wraps her big, black, pillowy arms around Riley and kisses him on the cheek. "Don't worry, old man," she says. "I'll keep you warm." Riley laughs and winks at me.

I giggle. "See you lovebirds later."

There's still some time before dinner, so I head to Sweet Bramble Books. It's the book and candy shop my grandmother owns, my favorite place in Bramble. Give me a good book and a bag of candy and I'm a happy camper.

The sun has long since burned away the fog.

Smiley-face pansies—purple, red, and yellow—
nod at me from the window boxes along Main
Street. Bramble is one of Cape Cod's original sea-
port villages. We still have some cobblestone
streets. Most of the buildings are brick or white
with clapboard shutters, some have plaques that
read, NATIONAL REGISTER OF HISTORIC PLACES.
Bramble United Community, we call it BUC,
stands tall at one end of Main Street. Bramble Free
Library, all covered with ivy, waves back from the
other end. In between are clothing shops and
restaurants; a two-screen movie theater; some
tacky tourist shops; the Town Green, where we
have concerts in the summer; Fancy's Fish Market;
Earl's Hardware; the new Sea Spa, where Tina and
Ruby get their beauty treatments; two art galleries;
Wickstrom's Jewelers, where JFK bought my heart
locket; the post office; the bank; Hairs to You,
where my hairdresser, Jo, designed my new one-
side-curly, one-side-straight hair; Miller's
Pharmacy; Cohen's Card Shop; Delilah's Florist;
Bloomin' Jean's Ice Cream Parlor; a two-for-one
T-shirt store; and . . . *ahhhhh* . . . my favorite store
in the world, Sweet Bramble Books.

The bells on the door jingle as I open it. Scamp

runs, happy to greet me. "Good dog," I say, giving him a hug. Scamp licks my face. Nana looks up from the candy counter.

"Willa, good, you're just in time. Come have a chocolate-covered strawberry. The berries aren't in season yet, but my produce supplier gave me a crate this morning."

I bite into the warm milk-chocolate jacket. "Delicious, Nana." Sweet strawberry juice dribbles down my chin.

"Remember when you used to love chocolate-covered cherries?" Nana says. "You always told me to leave the pits in the center for good luck."

"Then I ate so many I got sick of them."

Nana laughs. "That's okay. Tastes change. Now you're my chief saltwater taffy tester."

Cape Cod is famous for its saltwater taffy, in every flavor you could wish for.

Over on the book side of the store Muffles meows and leaps down from her sunny window perch. When Gramp Tweed was alive, every Friday he would leave a new book for me on that window ledge. Muffles would sit on it until I came.

It was just this past December that Gramp died of a heart attack. We all miss him like crazy,

Nana especially. She still has some really bad days. Though she is never the one to feel sorry for herself, never wants us to worry about her. But I do. Nana has had heart trouble of her own. I keep reminding her to take a walk every day.

Muffles meows, rubs her gray coat against my leg, circles around me, and meows again. I pick her up and scratch under her neck the way Gramp did. I rub my nose against her tiny wet nose. I bet Muff misses Gramp too.

"Did you hear Mom and Sam's news?" I ask.

"About the baby?" Nana says, looking at me over the bridge of her glasses.

I nod.

"Yes. Stella called me this morning." Nana doesn't sound pleased. She shakes her head and sighs. "That daughter of mine never ceases to surprise me. What is she thinking of? A baby at her age?"

"But Nana, Mom only just turned forty. Lots of women have—"

"I know, I know, but the older you are, the greater the risks of something going wrong and . . ."

"Nothing will go wrong," I say. "My mother is the healthiest person I know. She's strictly vegetarian now, and she jogs five—"

"Jogs blogs," Nana says. "Stella better slow down. And forget the vegetables. She better start eating some good American Angus beef, or she won't be getting enough protein. And how is she going to run an inn and take care of an infant and . . ."

I walk away so Nana can rant and rave in peace. Let's just say Nana and Mom don't always see the world through the same pair of sunglasses.

There's a new display of books on the main table. *Our Town* by Thornton Wilder. I pick up a copy and read the back jacket:

Our Town was first produced and published in 1938 to wide acclaim. This Pulitzer Prize-winning drama of life in the small village of Grover's Corners, an allegorical representation of all life, has become a classic.

Sounds good.

You are holding in your hands a great American play. Possibly *the* great American play.—Donald Margulies
It touches the soul like a miracle.—Albert Einstein

The Albert Einstein? Wow.

I grab two more chocolate-covered strawberries and plop down on the old tweed couch. Gramp and I used to sit here and "book-talk" every Friday afternoon after school. I open *Our Town* to act 1:

"This play is called 'Our Town.' . . ."

A long while later I'm still reading. There are chocolate smudges on the pages. I don't want to put the book down.

"You should try out," Nana says.

"Try what out?"

"The play. *Our Town.* Upper Cape Repertory is holding auditions—a week from next Friday, I think it is. My friend Gail George dropped off those flyers on the counter. That's why I ordered in the books."

"Mmmmm, maybe. Can I keep this copy?"

"Of course. Any book you ever want. Gramp always said you were his best customer."

I give Nana a hug. She smells like lavender. "Are you doing okay, Nana?"

"Fine as I can, honey. Day by day."

"You're getting out for your walks, right? And you're taking your heart medication, right?"

"Willa, you are such a worrywart." Nana shakes

her head, laughing, pushing me toward the door. "Go home now, but come back this weekend, I need you to rate some new taffies for me. Summer's coming and I've got to be ready."

I take a yellow flyer off the counter and stick it inside *Our Town*. I fill a bag with my current favorite flavors of saltwater taffy: lemon lime, chocolate, and peppermint.

"Thanks for the book, Nana, and the candy." I hug her again.

"Anytime, honey. Anytime."

Our guests are having cocktails and hors d'oeuvres on the front porch when I get home. I grab a small plate of cheese and crackers and a handful of grapes and sneak up to my room. I finish reading *Our Town*. I know whom I want to play.

Emily. She's the star of the show. She loves her town the way I love Bramble. Everyone is so kind and good to one another. Emily is the smartest girl in her school, and she's in love with a boy named George Gibbs. She tells him, "All I want is someone to love me." And he says, "I will, Emily." And she says, "And I mean for *ever*. Do you hear? For ever and ever." And then the next scene is their wedding day.

It's just so perfectly romantic. I want that part. I am perfect for that part.

Now, if only JFK will play George. . . .

CHAPTER 5

Entire Towns of Butterflies

*Is there no one in town aware of social injustice
and . . . inequality?*
*Oh, yes, everybody is. . . . Seems like they spend
most of their time talking about who's rich and
who's poor.*

—*Our Town*

"April break is turning into a nightmare," Ruby
Sivler complains to me and Tina at lunch on
Monday. "An absolute nightmare."

"You're going to Mexico, right?" Tina says,
looking all concerned.

"No-o," Ruby says. "Well . . . yes . . . we *were*.
Mommy booked us four deluxe beachfront suites
at the brand-new Grand Highness Royale in

Cancún. She booked them last July. *Last July.* That's how long ago she booked them. . . ."

Four beachfront suites. It's just Ruby and her sister, her mom and dad. They each need their own suite?

"And then some storm hit last month and destroyed the entire beach. All the cute little striped cabanas, the palm trees . . . I guess the waves washed right up and ruined all three pools and the hot tubs, too. Can you imagine?"

"Hurricane Igor," I say, "it was awful. Lots of people lost their—"

"Well, anyway," Ruby says, cutting me off. "Thankfully our travel agent has connections, and she was able to book us back to Grand Cayman Island. We were just there last year, so it'll be *boring*, but at least I'll get my spring tan."

"Thank goodness for that," I say.

Tina looks at me and rolls her eyes.

Tina's right. Ruby is harmless. It's just that she also seems to be totally clueless about the real world. People lost their houses, their businesses, some lost their *lives* in that hurricane, and all Ruby can think about is how it inconvenienced her *vacation*?

I can tell Tina sympathizes with Ruby. They have a lot in common. They used to be best friends before I moved to Bramble. Tina's rich too. Her family always goes someplace tropical every holiday break, winter break, spring break. . . . My family is middle class. Although Sam says we're rich by world standards. He's always cutting out articles in the paper about countries where children have to beg for food or where mothers have to walk for days with babies strapped on their backs just to fill jugs with clean water. It's like Mum was trying to tell me. The job is never done. There is always another way to help make the world a better—

Tina elbows me hard. "Look," she whispers.

JFK is heading toward our table. I finger the chain of the locket around my neck.

"Come on, Ruby," Tina says, standing, trying to block Ruby's view of JFK. "Let's get dessert. They've got fudge fancies today."

"Ooh, yummy," Ruby says.

I don't even have time to worry about my hair or anything before JFK sits down across from me. "Hey," he says, and smiles.

"Hi, Joseph."

"You're wearing it, huh?"

"Yep." Why do I still feel like entire towns of butterflies are hatching in my stomach every time I see him? We're a couple now. When does it get less scary?

"Do you want to do something Saturday?" he says.

"Sure."

"Like what?"

Anything. Anything. Dinner, a movie, watching the clock tick . . .

"I don't care, whatever. How about you?"

"Maybe we could hit the beach for a while, grab a pizza at Zoe's after?"

Butterflies be gone. I take a leap. "How about if I make us a picnic? It's supposed to be warm all week."

JFK smiles. My left hand holds my right hand down to resist touching that dimple. And those eyes, those eyes. Could they be any bluer?

"Sure, but I invited you," he says. "What do you want me to bring?"

Yourself. Those peppermint lips . . . "How about dessert?"

He laughs. "I don't know. That might be out of my league."

"A Frisbee maybe?"

"Frisbees I can do. I'll bike to your house around two. Good?"

"Good."

Oh, yes, very good. Very, very good.

After dinner I look for Sam. He's in his study on the third floor. It's a small yellow room, lined with books from floor to ceiling, with a narrow stairway leading up to the widow's walk. Years ago wives would pace back and forth up there, hoping to spot their husband's ship. The seafaring life was harsh, though, and many men never made it home.

The door is ajar. Sam is at his desk, writing furiously fast. Catching fireflies, I bet. That's what we call those moments of inspiration when words are coming fast and free in our heads, and we have to catch them *quick, quick*, like lightning bugs in a mayonnaise jar, before they fly away.

I stand patiently in the hall, waiting. I'm curious to know what Sam is writing, but I won't interrupt a moment like this. When Sam first showed me and Mom this room on their first official date, he said he was working on a book. He hasn't mentioned it since. I peek back in again, then again.

When Sam finally stops writing, I knock.

"Willa, hi, come in." Sam closes the notebook and slides it into the top drawer. He doesn't want to tell me what he's working on. "What's up?"

I tell Sam how I'm searching for a new cause for our class. Saving the Bramble Library was good, but now it's time to move on. And where to begin? So many bad, sad things in the world. So many people to help . . .

"Willa," Sam says, eyes shining. "I'm proud to be your . . . *in your* family."

I know he was going to say "proud to be your father." Just wait until June, Sam.

"It really doesn't matter what you choose," he says. "I imagine you are going to do many important things in your life. This is just the next way you'll make the world a little better. We are so lucky here in America, not all Americans, but us, our family, we are healthy, fed, educated. We are even lucky to have the luxury of looking around to wonder how we can share a bit of the goodness we've been given."

"But Freshman Class Meeting is Friday, and I'd like to have a proposal."

"Anything you do will be more than has been there before."

"I don't want to ask people for any more money. . . ."

"Forget about money," Sam says. "Money is a Band-Aid. People connecting with people is where the real good stuff happens. Person to person. Teaching someone how to read. Helping someone find a job. . . ."

"But Sam, where do you begin?"

"Inside. Listen to your own voice, Willa. I always find that if I shut up long enough and listen, the answer comes."

I am dying to ask Sam what he's writing, but I respect that if he wanted to tell me, he would. "Thanks, Sam, good night."

"Night, Willa, sweet dreams."

"Oh, wait, Sam, what are we reading next in class?"

"Follow the yellow brick road."

"*The Wizard of Oz*?" I laugh. "Isn't *Oz* a little young for high school? We've been studying Shakespeare all year with Dr. Swaminathan."

"And that's wonderful. But I don't know when I'll get another chance to teach literature again, so

I thought I'd do some personal favorites."

"But Dorothy and Toto, Sam? What's to study? Everybody knows the story."

"Actually, many people only know the movie version. The original book by L. Frank Baum is brilliant in its simplicity. I think it is the finest, uniquely American fairy tale. The quintessential journey theme, searching for the thing we think we want most, trying to find a way back home . . ."

That night I write in my journal. "On June 18, for the first time ever, I will say 'Happy Father's Day, Dad.'"

Dad, Dad, Dad.

Sam will be so happy.

CHAPTER 6

The Mystery Girl

Oh, earth, you're too wonderful for anybody to realize you.

—Emily, *Our Town*

I love *Our Town*. I love Emily. I have to get the part.

There I am on the stage, a hush falls over the theater, the audience dabbing tears, leaning forward to catch each beautiful word:

"'Good-by, Good-by, world. Good-by, Grover's Corners . . . Mama and Papa. Good-by to clocks ticking . . . and Mama's sunflowers. And food and coffee. And new-ironed dresses and hot baths . . . and sleeping and waking up. . . .'"

I already have half the lines memorized.

"You're trying out for a play?" Tina asks, all excited. "Oh, me too, me too."

For as long as I've known Tina, it's been her dream to be a soap star. I didn't think she was interested in the theater. "Do you even know the story?" I ask.

"No, but I'll read it tonight. How hard can it be? When are auditions?"

"Next week." My heart is pounding. I don't want Tina to try out. Nana's friend Gail George said the director wants to cast the entire play with young, teenage actors. Tina might not get all the subtle nuances of the play, but she's gorgeous and dramatic. What if she wins the director's heart with her charm?

I want to be Emily.

"The stage is different from television, Tina. In the theater you are right there, a stone's throw from the audience, so close you can reach out and touch them. You have to be totally into character. It's all about the story. It's the truest interpretation of the writer's actual—"

"Well, excuse me, Willa." Tina crosses her arms in front of her chest and flips her angel hair back, case closed. "Don't get your big book brain all bent out of shape. You don't think I can do it, do you?"

"I didn't say that."

"Don't you remember, Willa, after we wowed them at that town council meeting, Dr. Swammy said we gave a brilliant performance. He said we should both try out for the spring—"

"This isn't some cheesy Bramble Academy production, Tina. This is *Upper Cape Repertory*. . . ."

Tina giggles.

"What?"

"Upper Cape Repertory. Sounds like a contagious disease." Tina puts a fist under her chin like a microphone and makes her voice deeper. "Attention, ladies and gentlemen, we interrupt our usual broadcast with a special report . . . stock up on tissues and nasal spray, we have a serious *upper cape repertory problem* on our hands. . . ."

"Cut it out, Tina."

Sometimes I wonder how we are best friends. We are so different.

When I stop by the Bramble Library to tell Mrs. Saperstone I'm auditioning for the role of Emily Webb in *Our Town*, her face gets gushy like she's going to cry.

"*Our Town*. I love that play. You would be the

perfect Emily, Willa. Or, the Stage Manager. I actually think the Stage—"

"No. I want to be Emily."

And on our date Saturday maybe I can talk JFK into auditioning for George Gibbs. Emily Webb and George Gibbs get married in the play.

"Well, either part, Willa, really any role would be wonderful. I think it's probably my favorite play ever . . . oh, wait, lest I forget. I've got two books for you."

Now that Gramp is gone, I rely on Mrs. Saperstone—and Sam, of course—for recommendations. Life is getting busier and busier with school and soccer and helping at the inn. I don't want to waste time on so-so stories. I want to read the best books. Gramp always said to read the good ones while you're young, because you may not have time when you're older. I'm beginning to see what Gramp meant.

Mrs. Saperstone hands me two books. "Quite a talented pair, those Brontë sisters. Emily wrote *Wuthering Heights* and Charlotte wrote *Jane Eyre.* They were both published right around the same time, if I'm not mistaken. . . ."

As Mrs. Saperstone talks, I move to look out the

window. The forsythia bush is in bloom, daffodils, tulips, grape hyacinths. Something moves behind the whale spoutin' fountain. I have a feeling like someone is watching me. I move to the far corner of the window and wait, one eye peeking out from the curtain folds. Sure enough, something moves again. Then I see her face, the girl from the beach. "Mrs. Saperstone, come quick. Do you know who that is?"

When Mrs. Saperstone reaches the window, the girl is gone.

"She's about this tall," I say, "really pretty, dark skin, long black curly hair. . . ."

Mrs. Saperstone's face lights up with a smile. "That sounds like Mariel Sanchez. She's new in Bramble. You two should meet, Willa. You'd like her."

I feel a cold stab of jealousy. *No. I don't like her, and I don't want you to either.*

"Isn't Mariel such a pretty name?" Mrs. Saperstone says. "I looked it up. It means 'sea bright.' Isn't that lovely? Sea bright."

Sea bright, my butt. Sea hag, maybe, sea monster.

"Mariel's in here all the time," Mrs. Saperstone babbles on. "I'm pretty sure she's homeschooled.

She comes in every afternoon around one o'clock. And what a voracious reader. She gobbles up books like us, Willa. And she's not afraid to tackle the tough ones. You two would have a lot to talk about."

"You've got that right," I mumble.

"So you already know each other?"

"No, not really."

"Well, I'd be happy to introduce you when—"

"No, that's okay, Mrs. S. Thanks for the books."

"Sure. Good luck with the tryouts, Willa. Keep me posted."

I turn to leave.

"You know what," Mrs. Saperstone says, "I just remembered. Mariel is reading *Our Town* too."

"Well, isn't she special."

Mrs. Saperstone looks surprised.

"I'm sorry. That's nice."

First my beach. Then my boyfriend. Now my books, too.

Who is this strange girl, anyway?

CHAPTER 7

The Other Side of Bramble

Everybody has a right to their own troubles.

—Our Town

Outside the library I quickly scan up and down Main Street. There, two blocks up, I spot her. Head down, I start to follow.

Mariel Sanchez is far enough in front that if she doesn't turn around, she won't notice me. Just in case, I pull the hood up on my slicker and put my sunglasses on.

Mariel is walking slowly, like she's in no hurry at all. I follow her out of the center of Bramble, past the public elementary school, the high school, the gas station. My heart is pounding. My hands are sweaty. I feel like a spy.

Mariel keeps walking, farther and farther. I look at my watch. I'm late for home. Mariel turns. She's heading toward the water.

I should go home right now, but I'm curious. I've gone this far, it's hard to stop. I want to see where she lives.

Mariel turns onto one of the nicest streets in Bramble. Wow, does she live here? Big, old sea captain houses with wraparound porches and rolling green lawns where clans of families congregate in the summer, fancy cars lining the driveways.

But no, Mariel keeps walking. And I keep following.

Mariel walks with her head straight ahead, not turning to notice things. She doesn't even seem to acknowledge the people she passes by. How rude. A few seconds later when I face those same people, I say hello. We are very friendly here in Bramble.

Mariel struts by the legendary lilacs in front of the Captain Greenwall Inn, gorgeous, thick purple bunches hanging down like grapes in a vineyard. She passes by like she doesn't even see them. I could never resist smelling those lilacs. Mariel resists. Then, a few steps ahead, she stops and comes back, plucks off a few branches, and continues on her way.

When I reach the Captain Greenwall, I stick my whole face in the sweet, soft purple and breathe it in. Down on the pavement I see the tiny buds that fell when that strange girl broke off her bouquet in haste.

Mariel turns onto Surf Drive. For a few moments I can't see her. I walk faster to catch up. When I get to the corner, I spot her. She is walking quicker now. I pick up my pace too. Past a super-market, a pizza place. There aren't any houses on this strip. I follow her for what feels like another mile. Past the cemetery, a boarded-up building . . .

We are on the other side of town now. It's amaz-ing that this, too, is Bramble. Like the lamb and lion sides of the Spit. Connected, but so far apart.

There's an awful stench in the air. I see a sign for a refuse recycling plant.

Mariel takes another turn and I follow. Past an ugly apartment building, then a trailer park. I really should go back, but I've come this far. . . .

Then all of a sudden Mariel stops. She opens a mailbox, peers in, closes it. She moves on, and I follow until I am standing in front of the sign for the Oceanview Inn: TOURISTS WELCOME.

I know this place. It's not an inn at all. There is

no view of the ocean. No view of anything nice. The Oceanview is a dumpy, run-down motel. Tourists have long since stopped coming here. Paint peeling, shingles falling down, windows gray with dirt. Diapers and blue work shirts hang from a clothesline between two trees. A solitary swing dangles at on odd angle, one chain longer than the other. A rusted metal sliding board lies tipped over in the mud beside it.

Mariel knocks on a door and enters. Moments later she comes out with two small, dark-haired children, one clung to each hip. She goes to the next door, sets the children down for a moment, fumbles with a key, and then they go in. I count down the number of doors, number 6.

I can't believe she lives here. I helped Nana deliver food here last Thanksgiving morning. Poor people rent rooms by the month. It's just a step up from a homeless shelter, Nana said.

We brought turkey, mashed potatoes, and all the fixings. I counted five children in one room. I couldn't believe a whole family was living in that one crummy room.

"People can't afford apartments, let alone houses on Cape anymore, Willa. It's a big problem. There are all these low-paid workers, mostly doing jobs that support the tourist industry—cleaners, cooks, cashiers, gardeners. . . . But people can't support families on minimum-wage salaries, let alone ever buy a house or put their kids through college."

I should go. I know I should leave, but I am strangely curious to find out more about this girl. I inch my way down along the rooms—1, 2, 3, 4, 5—my heart pounding. I reach the window. The drapes are open.

This is wrong, an invasion of privacy. Just one quick peek. I know I shouldn't. I have no right. Just do it. Look quick.

The room is dark. Mariel is on the floor, kneeling, hands folded, head bowed in front of a dresser. There is a statue on the dresser, a candle flickering, a photograph of a woman with black, curly hair, a glass filled with lilacs. The dark-haired children are standing up in a playpen, watching Mariel intently with huge brown eyes. Two neatly made single beds, a lamp and a stack of books on the nightstand, a small refrigerator with a microwave on top. I hear Mariel mumbling, like she's praying. I turn away, ashamed.

A large red van pulls up. U ARE THE U IN UCADS is

written in bold letters across the side, UPPER CAPE ASSOCIATION FOR DISABLED CITIZENS underneath. The van stops, and a lady comes around and slides open the door. "Mr. Sanchez," she calls. Sanchez, that's Mariel's last name. The lady presses a button and a ramp slides out, making a beep-beep-beeping sound as it descends to the pavement.

When the ramp clunks down, a dark-skinned man in a wheelchair appears at the top. He looks about Sam's age. I see the strong muscles in his forearms as he wheels himself down the ramp. "Thanks, J.C.," he says, "see you tomorrow."

I turn quick to avoid him, but the man spots me. For a moment we just look at each other. His eyes are deep brown pools. They are the saddest eyes I've ever seen.

I turn and hurry home.

CHAPTER 8

Ding-Dong Ding-a-Ling Happy

*People are meant to go through life two by two.
'Tain't natural to be lonesome.*

—Our Town

"Willa, come up here," Mom shouts when I get home. She's in one of the small guest bedrooms. Maybe she's thinking about converting it into a nursery for the baby.

"Guess who's getting married," she says, all excited.

"Who?"

"Guess. You'll never guess."

"I don't know, Mom, who?" And then I picture Sulamina Mum. Riley and Mum. I'd be so happy for them, but what if they decide to move back home? . . .

"Give up?"

"Yes."

"Suzanna Blazer! She just got engaged, and she wants to have the wedding here!"

I start to laugh. "That's wonderful!"

Suzanna Jubilee Blazer—we call her Suzy-Jube—is the gorgeous daughter of our best and nicest customers, Chickles and Bellford T. Blazer. A date with Suzy-Jube was the prize that lured all of the boys in Bramble to our Valentine's dance. Let's just say Suzy-Jube is a boy magnet. She has won a ton of beauty pageants. She was just crowned Miss American Role Model. "That's great, Mom. Who is she marrying?"

"His name is Simon Finch, and he's a drummer in a band—country music, I think—I forget the name. Suzy met him on her Miss Daisydew USA tour last year. Chickles says Simon 'doesn't have two nickels to tape together for a dime,' which I guess means he's not rich, but the Blazers don't care. They're millionaires. All they care about is that Suzy is happy. Chickles said she's never seen two people so much in love. They are, I think she said, 'ding-dong ding-a-ling happy,' and they want to tie the knot as soon as possible. They've booked the entire inn for the second Saturday in June, the tenth. The rehearsal dinner will be the night before, of course. I'm going to have to rebook the reservations we already have for that weekend, but—"

"*This June*? Two months from now? Why the hurry?"

"Simon's band is going on tour. . . ."

"Well, good for them. I'm happy for them."

"Me too," Mom says. She walks over to the window and looks out. "I was actually thinking lately that it might be time to start hosting more weddings here at the Inn." She turns and looks at me with an odd expression on her face and then turns back to the window. "The labyrinth and gardens are so beautiful, and now that the barn is all renovated, with the right lighting and flowers it would make a quaint chapel, and we could do something with fountains on the lake, white tents on the lawn for the reception. I know it's a lot to take on with a new baby on the way and . . ."

My heart beats harder. "Mom?"

She turns and smiles at me. She knows what I'm going to say.

"Can I please help you plan Suzanna's wedding?"

"Yes. I would love that, Willa." She walks over and touches my arm. "I know we got off to a rough start the first time. But we're both older and wiser now and . . ."

"Partners?" I say.

"Partners," she says.

I hug her tight and the tears come. Happy tears, both of us.

After dinner I finish my homework and call Tina.

"Wait until you hear this. We're back in the wedding-planning business. And this time Mom and I are going to be partners."

"Whoopee!" Tina says. "That's great. Now, Willa . . ." Her voice gets more serious. "This is important, so listen. You better get online right now and start researching. Keeping track of what's in and out for weddings is like keeping track of shoe styles. If you miss a week, you're dead. The last thing you want to do is plan some old-fashioned . . ."

Tina dreams of the day she'll say "I do." She already has an album filled with pictures of wedding gowns and bridesmaids dresses, destination wedding packages . . .

"You'll need a signature cocktail, of course," Tina says.

"A what?"

Tina sighs. "Oh, Willa, please, don't you read the celebrity magazines? Anybody who's anybody has a fancy drink, a signature cocktail, created especially for their wedding."

"What about champagne—"

Tina sighs louder. "Willa, please, champagne is *soooo* last season."

Later I open my journal and start to write. So many good things are happening at once. JFK . . . *Our Town* . . . a baby on the way . . . and now Suzanna's wedding!

I've been keeping a chronicle of my life since September of eighth grade, when I inadvertently caused my wedding-planner mother's most famous wedding, two stars from *Forever Young*, to end in a disaster. I was actually trying to do something good for the bride and groom, but my best intentions backfired into a colossal disaster that made headlines nationwide and resulted in Mom deciding to give up Weddings by Havisham and move us to Maine to live.

The day we left Bramble was the saddest day of my life, but my wonderful friend Mr. Tweed—this was before he married Nana and became Gramp Tweed—gave me a journal. It had a brown cover with a sunflower on the front. I poured out all of my anger and sadness into that blank book, and every time I wrote, I felt better.

When we moved back to Bramble, I bought myself a new journal, and then another and another. They are lined up in chronological order on the top shelf of my bookcase, right there with my Willa's Pix, my very favorite books in the world. I don't write every day, but I do try to catch the highlights. When I look back and read old entries it reminds me what was in my heart then, what I was worried about, or excited about, what I cared about, what I loved.

I can't believe we are getting back in to the wedding-planning business. *How fun.* All those years when my mother ran Weddings by Havisham, she pushed away every man who might want to marry her, and she locked me out of her wedding-planning world. I guess she worried that if I got too wrapped up in dreamy, fairy-tale wedding stuff that I would spend less time on school.

It has always been important to her that I get good grades and set my sights on college. I was actually forbidden from going into her studio, but I had a key and would sneak down at night to see the easels, which displayed the Twelve Perfect Ingredients of whatever masterpiece wedding she was working on at the time, quietly adding my own thirteenth secret ingredient. . . .

Now Mom is happily married to Sam and they are going to have a baby and we live in a gorgeous inn and I have a wonderful father and one of my favorite people in the world is getting married and I am going to help plan her wedding!

I open *Our Town* and stand in front of the mirror. I stare at the girl looking back at me. Curly hair on one side, horse-tail straight on the other, blue eyes, my one and only really good feature. Skinny body, like a ten-year-old. I turn to act 1. Emily is talking to her mother.

EMILY: Mama, will you answer me a question, serious?

MRS. WEBB: Seriously, dear—not serious.

EMILY: Seriously,—will you?

MRS. WEBB: Of course, I will.

EMILY: Mama, am I good looking?

MRS. WEBB: Yes, of course you are. All my children have got good features; I'd be ashamed if they hadn't.

EMILY: Oh, Mama, that's not what I mean. What I mean is: am I *pretty*?

MRS. WEBB: I've already told you, yes. . . . I never heard of such foolishness.

EMILY: Oh, Mama, you never tell us the truth about anything.

I finish all the lines from act 1, then move on to act 2. Auditions are a week from Friday. I just have to get this part. I just have to be Emily.

I pull out the bag of taffy from my nightstand, open up a peppermint one, and pop it in. Mmmm, good. Which book tonight? *Wuthering Heights* or *Wizard of Oz*?

I pick the yellow brick road.

CHAPTER 9

Come Home Cape Cod

I'm going to make speeches all my life.

—Emily, *Our Town*

By Thursday afternoon I still haven't come up with a good idea for our next Community Service project, and Freshman Class Meeting is tomorrow.

"How about a race for the heart association?" Mom suggests. "Maybe in Gramp's memory." My mother runs 5K and 10K road races to raise money for various charities.

Mrs. Saperstone has another thought. "Maybe your class could become literacy volunteers," she says. "It only takes a few weeks to learn how to teach someone to read. It would be a perfect follow-up to your campaign to save the library. We do the training right here, and a new session is starting soon."

"How about a book drive?" Sam suggests. "A lot of schools lost everything in that hurricane down South last month," Sam says. "Maybe you could collect books to restock a school library. That would be a fine contribution."

On Friday morning I'm in the kitchen making tea when I see Rosie's paycheck on the counter next to her purse. I shouldn't look. It's none of my business, but I do.

What? That's all Rosie makes for a whole week working here? That's less than Tina spends on clothes in a week.

I go and find my mother. "Why don't we pay Rosie more?"

Mom raises her eyebrows. "How do you know what we pay Rosie?"

I tell her how I snooped, but that isn't the point.

"It's none of your business, Willa," Mom says, "but that's actually several dollars above minimum wage. Rosie doesn't have a college degree and—"

"Why does that matter? She's an awesome cook, especially desserts. She should have her own bakery or something. So what if she doesn't have a degree? How is she supposed to take care of Liliana and buy a house for them and put her through college someday—"

"Whoa, Willa. A house?" My mother lowers her voice, looks around to make sure no guests are nearby. "Rosie's lucky she can afford an apartment. She's lucky she has this job."

"You mean Liliana is never going to have her own house? A yard with a swing set and a sliding—"

"Willa." Mom smiles. "You have such a good heart. It's wonderful you care so much, but . . . hmmm, wait, you made me think of something. I was just reading in the paper about a new organization called Come Home Cape Cod. Yesterday's paper, I think. They are raising money to build houses for low-income Cape Cod families."

That's it. "That's great, Mom, thanks!"

I go up to my room to do some research. I find the article about Come Home Cape Cod in the *Cape Cod Times*. JFK's father is the publisher. Maybe he knows more about it. The story talks about how finding affordable housing has become a serious problem on Cape Cod. Developers are swallowing up land and building expensive vacation homes, while many people who grew up here are being forced to move off Cape because they can't afford to live here anymore.

Come Home Cape Cod hopes to build ten homes a year. It says it costs about $50,000 to build one of these houses, but if they can get land donated and contributions of materials from building companies and free labor from roofers and electricians and other services, it can cost less.

I find information on the numbers of Cape Codders who are living in poverty and about what the average Cape Cod worker makes and how many people are living in temporary shelters, places like the crummy Oceanview Inn. . . .

This is going to be great.

When I share my idea at Freshman Class Meeting, though, let's just say I don't get a standing ovation.

"Oh, Willa," Ruby Sivler says, "give it a rest, will you? We did the library. Isn't that enough? It's almost summer. Time to think about pool parties and beach parties and boat trips to Nantucket and the Vineyard and . . . well . . . I don't want to feel all sad and guilty about poor people. I mean, my mother and father give money. They are, like, the biggest contributors to the Cape Cod Symphony and . . ."

I look over at the boys. Jessie has his headset on. Luke's playing a video game. JFK smiles at me. He shrugs. "I think it's a great idea," he says, "but fifty thousand dollars is a lot of money."

"It doesn't all have to be in cash," I say. "We can get businesses to contribute, someone to give us the land, a lumber company to supply the wood. And we can all help on-site with the actual building."

"You mean with hammers and nails?" Tina says. She scrunches her nose, then sighs loudly. "I know you mean well, sweetie, but I agree with Ruby. It just sounds like an awful lot of . . . *work* . . . to me. Nobody's making us do this, right? I mean, we all got our twenty-five hours with the library thing, right?"

Every student at Bramble Academy is required to do twenty-five hours of community service during each of our four years of high school. "Well, yes, technically we've all met this year's obligation, but—"

"Willa," Tina says, tilting her head at me like, *Come on, let it go*. "We're all really busy. . . ."

I look around at my classmates—Emily, Gus, Trish, Shefali. Nobody else seems interested either.

"Well, what about a 5K race for the heart association?" I say.

"Too much work, Willa," Ruby says.

"How about being literacy volunteers? It only takes a few weeks to train. . . ."

"Too much time, Willa," Tina says.

"Well then," I say, "what about collecting books to send to a school that lost its library in the hurricane?"

Ruby perks up. "You mean in Cancún?"

"No," I say. "In America."

"Now, that sounds just right," Tina says. "I've got books in the basement I'd be happy to throw . . . I mean . . . *give* away for a good cause."

The bell rings. "Okay, then, everybody," I say. "Show of hands. Who's in?" Everybody raises their hands. Tina pulls Jessie's hand off of his headset and holds it up in the air. He smiles at her. They are so in love.

Unanimous. "Okay, then, books it is. Let's start collecting today. I'll get permission to store them in the old gym. Try to get as many good children's books as you can find. Ask your relatives, your neighbors. The more the better . . ."

***

But I'm not done with Come Home Cape Cod.

When I get home, I write an editorial letter and e-mail it to the *Cape Cod Times*. I say that I'm a high school student here on Cape, a wash-ashore who feels like I was born here, and I love this place and the people who live here, and how I think it is wrong that some people who were born and raised here can't afford apartments, let alone a house, and that I just found out about the Come Home Cape Cod organization and that I hope anyone who can possibly contribute money or materials will do so. Give as much as they can, as soon as possible. I list the address and tele-phone number. *Thank you.*

Now I feel a little better.

After dinner I tell Sam what happened at the meeting. "You're a natural born leader, Willa. I'm proud of you. Maybe you'll be mayor or senator or *president* some day."

I laugh. "I thought you hated politicians, Sam."

"No, I'm just disappointed in the lack of vision in our country. There used to be leaders we could look up to and respect. People who inspired us. John F. Kennedy, Martin Luther King Jr. . . ."

"You mean Democrats, right, Sam?" Mother

and Sam are always arguing about politics. Sam is a Democrat. Mom's a Republican.

"I mean leaders, Willa, humanitarians who motivate people to look around and care about others. It was good that you wrote that letter. You never know who your words might inspire."

Later, when my homework is finished, I check through my book of famous quotations and head down to change the Bramble Board. There was once a young American president who loved Cape Cod. His family had a home here in Hyannis, and he walked the Cape beaches for inspiration. He was a big believer in community service. In one of his most famous speeches he called on every American to join in and do their part:

ASK NOT WHAT YOUR COUNTRY CAN DO FOR YOU, ASK WHAT YOU CAN DO FOR YOUR COUNTRY.

I stand back and read President Kennedy's words on the Bramble Board. Two new guests, the Carlsons from Connecticut, are coming up the driveway. They stop and read the quote. They smile and nod at me.

Back up in my room, I finish practicing act 3 of

Our Town. "'I can choose a birthday at least, can't I?—I choose my twelfth birthday. . . . Oh, I want the whole day.'"

I look out my window, up at the sky. The North Star, the Big and Little Dippers . . . I wish I could see a shooting star. In all the years I've searched the sky, I have never seen one. I imagine it must be beautiful and lucky.

After I write in my journal, I prop up my pillows, open my bag of taffy, wrap my quilt around me like a cape, and set out onto the foggy, whimsical, windswept moors of *Wuthering Heights.*

Heathcliff is so romantic.

CHAPTER 10

Beach Date

Try and remember what it was like to have been very young.
And particularly the days when you were first in love; when you were like a person sleepwalking, and you didn't quite see the street you were in, and didn't quite hear everything that was said to you.

—Our Town

Saturday is warm and sunny, perfect for my beach date with JFK.

I find my favorite shorts from last summer. Good thing, they still fit perfectly. Unfortunately, so does my favorite yellow T-shirt. I change into a white tank top with a blue chambray shirt over it, knotted in the front, slide on my red sneakers, comb the straight side of my hair and puff up the curly side, and put on sunblock, mascara, my cherry-flavored lip gloss, and then my locket.

I open the heart and look at the upside-down faces. Our school photos. Me on one side, JFK on the other. I close the heart and polish it shiny. Hopefully I can convince Joseph to try out for *Our Town*. How romantic would that be? Me in a wedding dress, him in a tux waiting for me at the altar.

Rosie is leaving for the day, but she stays to help me with the picnic.

"Are you sure you don't mind?" I ask.

"Not at all," Rosie says. "I hear your boy is quite a catch. I'd like to meet—"

"Oh, sure, Rosie, but not today, okay? This is our first official just-the-two-of-us date. Before, we've just met at Zoe's or something with Tina and Jessie. Today will be the parents interrogation day, and I don't want him to get too embarrassed."

"No problem, Willa," Rosie says. "Next time."

We wrap up thick pieces of barbecue baked chicken, a container of pasta salad, Cape Cod potato chips, peaches, rolls, soda, plates, forks, and knives. A wicker basket would be more romantic, but an insulated beach pack is more practical. "Get some sugar cookies," Rosie says. "I just stocked the jar. They're probably still warm."

Every afternoon from two to four is teatime at Bramblebriar. We keep a big blue jar filled with cookies for our guests to enjoy with hot or cold tea and coffee. Every day is a fresh new batch—chocolate chip, oatmeal raisin, Heath bar crunch. . . .

There are several guests hovering around the table. I make small talk and budge to the front as tactfully as I can. I do live here, after all.

Rosie hands me some pink cloth napkins. "Fancier than paper," she says.

"Thanks so much, Rosie."

"You're welcome, Willa. Have fun!"

The doorbell rings right at two o'clock. Mom and Sam are waiting in the vestibule.

"Mom," I say, nervous, catching a quick look in the hallway mirror. "Please just say hello and let us go, okay?"

She opens the door. "Hi, Joseph, come in."

JFK looks like he should be on the cover of *Cape Cod Life* magazine. Cut-off jean shorts hung low on his hips, white pocket T-shirt, sandy brown hair tucked behind his ear, a Frisbee under his arm. He looks tanned, like he's been out sailing all day.

An alarm bell wakes the towns of butterflies in my stomach, and they all start batting their wings at once. He is so beautiful.

"Hi, Willa." JFK cocks his head, shy. He turns the Frisbee around in his hand like he's steering it for support.

"Hi, Joseph." I set down the picnic bag. "I think you know my mother."

JFK shakes her hand. "Mrs. Gracemore, it's a pleasure."

"Nice to formally meet you, Joseph."

"And I know you know my stepfather, Sam Gracemore."

"Mr. Gracemore." JFK shakes Sam's hand. "I started *Oz* last night. It's good."

"Glad you like it, Joe," Sam says, smiling.

I pick up the picnic. "All set?"

"What time will you be home?" Mom asks.

"Is nine okay?" JFK says.

"That's fine," Mom says.

And then, thank all the angels in heaven, we're off.

JFK hooks the picnic bag onto the handlebars of his bike. I put a beach blanket and the Frisbee in the basket on mine. "Ready?" he says.

"Ready." And off we go to Sandy Beach.

The bike lane is narrow. JFK goes ahead of me. I follow along behind him, the sun on my face, wind whistling in my ears. I feel so happy and pretty and lucky. I picture us holding hands walking out on the Spit, eating dinner, kissing. . . . Then before I know it, we are pulling into the parking lot, setting our bikes in the rack. I don't remember one street we passed. It's like I dreamed myself here.

There are several people on the beach. It's warm. We walk down the steps and kick off our sneaks.

"Where should we put this?" JFK says, holding up the bag.

"Let's walk out a bit," I say. *I'd like to walk all the way out to that secluded little scallop of beach, our special spot, where you kissed me on the cheek in seventh grade. . . .*

"Good, let's go," he says, slinging the picnic sack on his shoulder.

I walk next to him. He lets me have the level ground by the water. The ocean is calm, there's a light, feathery breeze. The sky is the color I used to pick from the crayon box to paint the picture perfect when I was little.

We arc around a young boy and his mother building a sand castle. It's quite an elaborate affair, moat and everything. The boy unloads a cement-mixer pail of sand, complete with sound effects. His trusty assistant packs it smooth. Past them are some little girls. They hunker together and giggle as we go by. Farther out, a couple about Mom's and Sam's age are nestled in beach chairs, reading under a striped umbrella.

The woman looks up from her book and smiles at us.

Suddenly it strikes me. JFK and I aren't talking. We're just walking together, enjoying each other's company. And it doesn't seem strange at all.

"My father said you wrote a great letter about some organization trying to build houses for poor people," JFK says.

"Come Home Cape Cod," I say.

"My dad's giving it prime placement on Sunday's editorial page, setting it off in its own special box so it will really stand out."

"Tell him I said thank you. I hope it does some good."

We walk farther and farther along the Spit.

There's a man in a red kayak, two Sunfish

sailboats, a fishing rig far offshore.

"I'm sorry nobody was up for another big service project," JFK says. "Maybe next year."

"That's okay. I understand."

"But the book drive is a good idea. You've probably got enough books of your own to stock three or four school libraries." He smiles at me and we laugh.

"You too," I say. "Didn't you write on Tina's matchmaking survey that you couldn't pick just one favorite book."

As soon as I bring up that stupid survey, I regret it. I picture Mariel Sanchez. And what was she doing at the dance, anyway? And where did she get the gown and—

"Willa?"

"What?"

"Where are you?" JFK is staring at me.

"Oh, sorry." I laugh, and he laughs too.

We walk all the way out to the tip of the Spit. The wind picks up and whips my hair back. We turn the corner and there it is.

Our spot. Like our own private island. No one else is around. Good.

"Do you want to eat now?" JFK says, setting the pack down. "I'm hungry."

"Sure." I lay out the blanket, smooth down the corners. I take out the food, set out our plates. JFK opens cans of soda.

He bites into the chicken and chews. "This is great. Thanks."

"You're welcome, but I can't take credit for it. Rosie made it. Tuna fish is about the extent of my culinary talents."

"Tuna fish is good," JFK says, "nothing wrong with tuna fish."

A seagull lands a few feet away and hurry-stops-hurry-stops toward us, trying to figure out if we're going to share. "Get out of here," JFK says, laughing. He throws a piece of roll down the beach to shoo the bird away. I stare at his long, tanned arm, the yellow band on his wrist, LIVE STRONG.

"Have you written any new lyrics?" I ask. JFK writes rap music. He shared some of his rhymes with me. They're good. He says rap is "like poetry except it's music."

"Not really." He takes more chicken. "I'm pretty tied up with baseball."

"Have you ever done any acting?" I ask. "You know, a theater production?"

JFK laughs. "Where did that come from?" He

wipes barbecue sauce off of his chin. "All right, listen. Don't tell Jessie and Luke, or anybody, but when we lived in Minnesota, I did *Romeo and Juliet.*"

"Really? That's great. What part did you play?"

"Believe it or not, Romeo."

Believe it? Of course I can believe it. Oh, how I would have loved to be Juliet.

"Why?" he asks.

"I have a motive."

JFK smiles. "What's that?"

"Do you know the play *Our Town*?"

He doesn't, so I tell him all about it, especially about George Gibbs and Emily Webb. "It's supposed to be the greatest American play of all time. Auditions are next week, and I'm trying out, and I was hoping maybe you would too."

"Sure."

"Really?" That was easy.

"Sure, why not? And it will get my mom off my back. She's disappointed that I gave up piano lessons. Since I was little, she's always made me do something in the arts to balance out all of the sports, and I guess this counts for culture, right?"

"Oh, absolutely. Definitely culture. And Nana's

got copies of the play in the store."

"Great, I'll buy one tomorrow," he says.

My heart is pounding. *This is perfect.*

"Willa?"

"What?"

He looks over his shoulders, up and down the beach. "So if I get the part of George and you're Emily and we get married, do we kiss at the wedding?"

"That's what the script says."

"Good, we better practice."

Then he kisses me, and I'm so happy I fly away with the butterflies.

It's getting dark when we pack up the picnic stuff and start heading back.

"There's the first star," I say, pointing.

"Make a wish," he says.

So romantic.

CHAPTER 11

"Mare"

A star's mighty good company.

—*Our Town*

I dream about a glistening wedding cake. The miniature bride and groom figurines on top are swirling around and around, dancing, dancing. They turn and I see their faces. Me and JFK.

I wake up smiling and reach for my journal to read what I wrote last night. I want to be sure I captured all the magic. Dinner on our own private island, the wind on our faces, how we laughed, talked . . . kissed. Then the "first star I see tonight" twinkling above. "Make a wish," he said. *So romantic.*

I can't wait to tell Suzanna Jubilee. She and Chickles, her mother—Mama B., as she tells us to call her—are coming this afternoon to talk about wedding plans.

Downstairs in the kitchen, Mom and Sam are having their morning coffee. Mom is drinking decaf now that she's pregnant. She's not showing yet. It's still too early.

"We need a signature cake," I say.

"What?" Sam says, setting down his cup. He smiles at me.

"The Bramblebriar Inn needs its own special signature wedding cake."

"Excellent idea," Mom says. "One more way to brand ourselves . . ."

"What?" Sam says.

"To differentiate ourselves," Mom explains, "like the things we do to set the Bramblebriar apart from all the dime-a-dozen antiques and blue hydrangea bed-and-breakfast places around here."

Sam looks at me and rolls his eyes. I smile.

"You know," Mom continues. "Like our fresh cookies and tea at two, and the hors d'oeuvres and drinks at six, and the labyrinth and the Bramble Board . . ."

"Well, that's not why I started the Bramble Board, but . . . I love my business-minded wife," Sam says, leaning over to kiss her cheek.

"But what about the cake?" I say.

"It's a spectacular idea," Mom says.

"Good. I'll ask Rosie to start working on a recipe. Sweets are her specialty."

When we get home from Sunday service at BUC, I finish my homework, then begin thinking about our new Community Service project. Sulamina Mum has a teacher friend in Louisiana. Her school lost their whole library in the flood. I find a box to begin loading up. Riley offered to transport all of our boxes down South in a rental truck.

I stare at all of the books on my shelf, reading the titles, remembering. Finding books I can donate is harder than I imagined. The books in my bedroom library are my favorite, special Willa's Pix books. I can't part with any of these. It would be like giving away friends, Tina or Mum. Well, not that hard, but close.

I carry the box down to the inn library and start looking. I go from shelf to shelf, pulling out duplicates and dog-eared paperbacks and titles our guests will probably never read. When I finish, the box is full, but something isn't right.

I feel like I'm getting rid of leftovers, not giving a good Thanksgiving dinner. I want to send those kids good books, the best books.

Sweet Bramble Books.

"Oh good, Willa," Nana says when I enter the store. "I've got new flavors for you to try."

The store is nearly empty. In a few weeks it will be packed with vacationing tourists looking for beach reads and kids shoveling Swedish fish and malted milk balls out of the plastic bins. Some Bramble locals have no patience for the tourists. They can be loud and demanding. But I don't mind. I used to be a tourist myself. I remember how it feels to know you have only a week to cram in a summer of fun before you have to head back over that roller-coaster bridge. It can make you crazy trying to cram in all that fun.

Now I'm a wash-ashore. That's what they call people who weren't born on Cape but move here to live. I like being a wash-ashore. It has such a romantic ring, doesn't it? Except, of course, when Nana starts ranting about some new "big-money wash-ashore" building another "McMansion" and destroying another patch of Cape Cod.

"Here," Nana says, handing me a piece of salt-water taffy.

I undo the wrapper, pop it in, and chew. The smooth, sweet candy slides across my tongue, sticks to my molars. "Mmmmm, nice, Nana. Tastes like chocolate and strawberry."

"Exactly," she says. "Chocolate-covered strawberries. Is it a keeper?"

"It's a keeper, Nana. It's a winner."

"Good." She kisses me on the cheek, all excited. Nana has a long-running friendly battle with Gheffi's Candy Store for the title of Best Sweets on the Upper Cape in *Cape Cod Life* magazine. She took the title away from them, and they want it back. Gheffi's sends scouts over to see what new taffy flavors and fudge combinations Nana is dreaming up, and every few months I sneak in to Gheffi's to do some subtle sleuthing for our side.

When I tell Nana about our book project, she throws her hands up in the air like she's cheering at a Red Sox game. "Wonderful," she says. "I was waiting for the perfect time. And this is it. Come on, it's quiet. I've got something to show you."

She locks the register and motions for me to follow her to the basement.

I don't remember being down here before. So

many doors. Nana opens one, turns on a light. "Look."

Books. A closet filled with books, shelves and shelves of books.

"Wow," I say.

"And that's not all," Nana says, opening another door.

This closet too is filled with books.

She opens another and then another.

"And they are all children's books," Nana says, all excited. "*Good ones*. Gramp was . . ." Her voice catches. "Gramp was waiting for just the right opportunity to start a library somewhere. In fact, when we were in New York City just before he died, he was talking with a friend of ours about sending the books to a village in Kenya. . . ."

My throat tightens. "I miss him so much."

"I know, honey," Nana whispers in my ear. "Me too. Give me a hug, shmug."

We hear the bells jingle on the door upstairs. "A customer," Nana says. She takes my face in her hands and stares into my eyes. "You take the books, Willa, and you carry on Gramp's dream. Okay? He'd be so proud of you. *I* am so proud of you."

I wipe my eyes and follow Nana upstairs.

My heart leaps.

It's JFK.

"Hi, Willa. Hello, Mrs. Tweed. I came to get *Our Town*."

After JFK buys the book and Nana gives him a complimentary quarter pound of chocolate pecan fudge, still warm from the pan, and a bag of sour gummy worms for his little brother, Brendan, JFK says he'll walk me home.

I tell him about the basement full of books and how the Blazers are coming later today to plan Suzanna's wedding, and then we turn the corner and nearly bump into Mariel Sanchez.

Her long black ringlets frame her beautiful, heart-shaped face. She's wearing a jean skirt, a low-cut white tank top, and a necklace made of beach glass—brown, blue, and green. She looks exotic, tropical.

"Joe," she shouts. Then she hugs my boyfriend, chest to chest, tight.

JFK coughs and pulls away. "Hi, Mare."

Mare? He calls her by a nickname?

"How are Nico and Sofia?" JFK asks awkwardly.

The two little kids, maybe? How does he know them?

"Fine," she says. She looks at me. "I'm Mariel Sanchez."

"Yes. We met on the beach last week." I reach for the locket, framing the heart with my thumb and pointer finger to be sure she sees it. "I was the one calling to you. I thought you had drowned or something." I look at JFK. I twist the heart back and forth, hoping the silver catches the sun, wanting to be certain she notices.

If she does, she doesn't let on at all. "Drowned?" Mariel laughs, a lilting sound like a chickadee. "What would make you think that? I was swimming." She reaches toward JFK. Takes the book from his hand. *"Our Town,"* she says with a sweet-sad smile. "I didn't know you—"

"What time is it?" JFK says, taking the book back, looking at his watch. "Oh, wow, I've got to go. Baseball practice. If I'm late, Coach'll make me do laps."

"Okay, sure," I say, turning to watch him leave. "Call me."

When I turn back around, Mariel is gone.

CHAPTER 12

Sixteen Bridesmaids

It seems to me that once in your life . . . you ought to see a country where they don't talk in English and don't even want to.

—*Our Town*

"*I was swimming.*" Mariel's words scratch like a sand flea in my head as I hurry home. The nerve of her to laugh at me. And the way she smiled at JFK, my boyfriend. *My boyfriend.* And how do they know each other? I need to talk to Tina.

But that will have to wait. The Blazing Buick limousine is in our driveway. *Beep, beep, beep.*

The back door of the limo flies open before the chauffeur can do his job, nearly knocking the poor guy out cold.

"Willa, honey!" Suzanna Jubilee shrieks, running toward me in a hot pink minidress. I brace myself for the tackle. We jump up and down, hugging, laughing.

"Congratulations, Suzy. I'm so happy for you!"

"My turn! My turn! Come here, baby," Mama Blazer says, swooping me up off my feet. "Gosh, we've missed you," she says, planting a big, slurpy kiss on my cheek.

She sets me down and swooshes back one of her signature feather boas, this one fire-engine red. "Let me look at you." She shakes her head side to side. "Cute as a button, pretty as a picture."

There's that *c*-word again.

"Willa, I have something to ask you," Suzy-Jube says. "Something important."

"Sure, anything."

Suzy looks at her mother. Her mother smiles and winks. Suzy looks at my mother. My mother smiles and winks.

"Willa," Suzy says, then pauses."Will you be my maid of honor?"

"Me?"

"You." Suzanna clasps her hands together, fingertips touching her lips, eyes squinting like, *I hope you'll say yes.*

I swallow hard. My eyes fill up. I've never been

in a wedding before. And the maid of honor . . . that's very special. "Are you sure?"

"Sure as sugar," Suzy says. "On Saturday, June tenth, Bramble, Cape Cod, United States of *A-mer-i-ca*, is going to have a wedding like it's never had before. I'm going to have sixteen bridesmaids. That's mine and Simon's lucky number. We met on September sixteenth and we counted sixteen stars on the night we first kissed, and well, I just couldn't leave any of my best, sweet pageant peeps, my chicklets, out of the wedding party, but then I couldn't pick one favorite to be my maid of honor, the rest would get all jealous, and so I thought about who I most wanted to have up there next to me on the stage on the most important day of my life, and your cute-as-a-button sweet little face popped right into my mind."

"Popped right in," Chickles says, testifying to the truth, crisscrossing her hands over her hefty chest.

"I'd be honored," I say.

"Good!" Suzy shrieks, and twirls me around. "Now, aren't you dying to see my man?" She reaches into her pocketbook and hands me a picture. "Willa Havisham, meet Simon Finch."

"Wow."

Simon Finch gives new meaning to the word "hot." Simon deserves his own new word. Long, dark hair, sultry eyes, stubble on his chin like he didn't shave that day, a leather choker with some sort of charm on it, a small hoop earring . . . Who cares if he doesn't have two nickels to tape together?

"He's gorgeous, Suzy. You make a stunning couple."

"Thanks, honey, I know. And he's just the perfect man for me. Isn't he, Mama?"

Chickles bobs her head like there has never been a truer true. "If Noah came back down again and called folks two by two, Suzy and Simon would be first on the ark."

I dig my fingernails into my palms so I won't giggle. I look quickly at Mom, but she's remaining nicely composed.

"And speaking of arks," Chickles continues, "we've rented out the new *Cape Queen* for the second reception. . . ."

"The cruise ship?" Stella says. "But don't you want to have the reception here?"

"Oh, yes, Stella. We want the wedding here, of

course, and the first reception for close family and friends. But we've got so many relatives and employees and business associates, and well, Suzanna has a ton of girlfriends from all her pageants, and Papa B and I thought it might be nice to invite all those nice young people we're putting through college through the Blazer Benevolent Foundation ever since we read those inspiring words on Willa's Bramble Board last year and started doing all these good things with our money, and well, this is our one and only baby girl and she's only going to get married once and we can afford to do it, so why not?"

The Blazers are loaded. I mean they are billion-aire loaded. And you can't even hold it against them because they are the kindest, sweetest, most down-to-earth people you'd ever want to meet.

"That sounds wonderful," my mother says.

"And of course you'll all come on the *Queen* with us," Mama B. says. "Right?"

"Well, we'll have to see," Mom says. "Summer is a busy time for us. . . ."

"Mom, please," I say.

"Let me talk to Sam," she says. "If there is any way we can, we will. Now, let's talk about the wedding. Come, let's sit on the porch. I'll get us some iced tea."

We make a circle with our wicker chairs. "Go ahead, princess," Mama B. says, "tell Stella and Willa what you have in mind for the wedding."

"Well . . . ," Suzy-Jube says, "I had a dream." She closes her eyes and smiles, then opens them. "And I could see the whole thing picture perfect. . . . You know that lovely lake you've got back there?"

Mom and I nod.

"Well, in my dream the audience, I mean the guests, were all seated facing the water. And there was a boat out on one side of the lake. I was sitting in the center of it. And a man in a costume started rowing it. You know, like those ganolas they have in Italy. That's where we're going on our honeymoon. Italy. Neither of us has been, and we don't speak Italian, but who cares about talking on your honeymoon, right?" She giggles. "Anyway . . . over on the other side of the lake, at the very same moment, Simon was being rowed out on another ganola, and the two boats met in the center and . . ."

I force myself not to look at my mother. I'm remembering her Weddings by Havisham studio and the easels where she'd display the Twelve

Perfect Ingredients of her masterpiece weddings, and I'm afraid if our eyes meet, she'll start laughing or crying. I get a picture of those "ganolas" in my head and picture these hunky muscle-beach lifeguards rowing Suzy, *row-ee-o, row, row.* And where will the sixteen bridesmaids be? And I dig my nails in deeper.

"Oh, and . . . ," Suzanna continues, "I want tons of dancing. Tons and tons of dancing. Maybe you can hire that jazzy babe who ran the turkey dance you had in the barn last Thanksgiving."

"Shirley Happyfeet?" Stella asks.

"That's right," Suzanna says. "Happy feet. Happy feet all night long."

Stella and I take notes as Suzanna talks. I can tell my mother is exercising every ounce of self-control to just listen, open minded. What Suzanna is describing is a far cry from the work-of-art weddings Stella Havisham was known for. But I've got to hand it to my mother. That steely coat of armor she used to wear seems to be in permanent storage. She actually seems to be enjoying this.

"And I want pony rides and clowns for all my little cousins . . . ," Suzanna sails on.

My mother sets down her glass of tea quickly.

"And, wait . . ." Suzanna gets a new idea. "What about acrobats? You've got all those lovely tall trees. . . ."

Mom goes over the menu choices, and I explain how we are working on a Bramblebriar Inn signature wedding cake that will make its grand debut at Suzanna's wedding.

"Yummy-yum-yum-yum," Mama B. says, smacking her lips together like she can taste the frosting already. "Better make it a big one. Everybody in the family has a super-size sweet tooth. Never skimp on the suga' when the Blazers are in town."

"The signature cake was Willa's idea," Mom says. "I think she has my wedding planner genes." She sets her pen on the table and rests her hand on her stomach.

I smile, nodding slightly toward her stomach and then at our guests with an expression like, *Are you going to tell them?*

Mom smiles and winks at me. "Oh, and we have some news, ladies," Mom says. "It's early and we really aren't telling many people yet, but . . . Sam and I are expecting a baby."

"A baby!" Mama B. shouts.

"A baby!" Suzy-Jube shouts. They rush to hug my mother.

"Wait till Papa B. hears you've got a guppy in your tuppy," Mama B. says. "He can't wait to be a granddaddy. He'll be ordering dollhouses and rocking horses and train sets and . . . is it a boy or a girl?

"It's still too early. We don't know yet," Mom says.

"Oh, Willa, how wonderful," Suzy-Jube says, hugging me again. "You're going to be a big sister!"

CHAPTER 13

Fly, Mama, Fly

Some people ain't made for small-town life.

—*Our Town*

After our wedding-planning session, Suzy-Jube and I have a chance to talk, just the two of us. I tell her about Mariel Sanchez and how she and JFK were a perfect match at the dance and how JFK called her Mare when we ran into her outside Nana's store and how she's beautiful and how she hugged him—

"Okay, honey, hold it right there," Suzy says. She stands up and puts her hands on her hips. "Listen up, because this is important."

I lean in closer, all ears.

Suzy checks her gorgeous face in the mirror. Straightens a lock of hair. Turns around and looks at me. "I always found with boyfriends—and believe me, I've had a gazillion—that the best thing to do is play your hand straight up. Lay your cards right on the table, no bluffin', and tell the boy you expect the same. And Willa, don't go getting worry wrinkles over the fish girl."

"The fish girl?" I laugh.

"What?" Suzy laughs too. "She sounds awful fishy to me, out swimming when any sensible girl would be home getting her beauty sleep. And . . . we can't jump to conclusions until we know the facts. Only Joey knows the facts. Now, here's what you do. There might not be anything to worry about a'tall. Don't make it into a soap opera or anything, just say real nonchalantly, 'Hey, Joe, how did you know that girl we saw the other day?' Now, listen, here's the key part. Don't look at him while you're talking. Be fixing your lipstick or brushing a crumb off the table or something, so it looks like you're hardly even listening, not concerned a'tall."

I have my chance the next day, when JFK sits with me in the cafeteria. Tina and Ruby are eating lunch outside, trying to catch some color. "Spring tan training," Ruby calls it.

JFK talks about the Red Sox.

They're looking good.

He talks about his baseball team.

They're looking good too.

I wait until just before the bell rings. I take out my new watermelon lip gloss and pull off the top. "Hey, Joseph, I was wondering. How do you know that girl we saw the other day"—I put on some gloss and smack my lips—"outside my grand-mother's store?" I put the top back on the tube. I brush a sandwich crumb off the table. Suzy-Jube would be proud.

"Uh . . ." JFK's face reddens. He crumples up his sandwich bag.

Oh, no. Not the reaction I was looking for.

"It's sort of awkward," he says.

Waves rush into my ears, drowning out his voice. "What do you mean 'awkward'?" I manage to say.

"I don't know if I should tell . . ."

My face flushes. Beads of sweat are forming on my forehead.

"What?" I say. "Tell me." *Please don't tell me you used to go out with her. . . .*

"Okay. We met last year in Hyannis. At a home-less shelter. I think I told you I used to go with my mom to volunteer sometimes. Well, one night when I was there, Mare came in with her baby brother and sister."

"Nico and Sofia?"

"Yeah, that's right. How did you know?"

"Never mind."

"Mare's father was in the hospital, and their landlord was a real jerk. He locked them out of their apartment because the rent was late. Mare was so embarrassed. 'We would have paid him back,' she said. My mother felt bad for them and sort of took Mare under her wing. She brought them clothes and diapers for the babies, helped Mare's father fill out paperwork for government assistance, even helped them find an apartment here in Bramble. . . ."

The bell rings.

"Where was Mariel's mother?" I ask.

"She's an actress," JFK says. "She had just landed a big role in some production that was touring the country. But Mr. Sanchez got hurt in an accident, and Mrs. Sanchez had to give up the play and come home. Mare said her mother got really depressed, I mean really depressed. Mare couldn't stand to see her so sad. And so she told her mother to go. Go back to the play, go follow her dreams. Mare said she'd take care of the babies."

JFK shakes his head. "Can you believe that? Being that brave? I mean, Mare is just a kid, and she said she'd be the mother so her mother could go be happy."

We walk to history class in silence. I feel an overwhelming sense of doom, like a thick curtain of fog is falling on my sunny little world.

Now I wish JFK had said, "Yeah, we went to the movies once." Or, "Yeah, we hung out at the mall." Or even, "Yeah, we used to go out." That I could deal with.

But no, this is bigger than that. Way bigger than that.

This girl is in his heart.

CHAPTER 14

Auditions

We've got a lot of pleasures of a kind here: we like the sun comin' up over the mountain in the morning, and we all notice a good deal about the birds. We pay a lot of attention to them.

—*Our Town*

I wake up the next morning with this queasy feeling inside. What if JFK cares more for Mariel than he is saying? What if they were more than friends? Why did she have to move here to Bramble, anyway? Hyannis is a perfectly good town. Why didn't her family stay there?

I pick up *Our Town*. Auditions are this Friday. I know Emily's lines by heart. I've practiced them on the beach, in front of the mirror, in the shower, in bed before I fall asleep. JFK says he's been practicing too. If all goes well, we'll be Emily and George.

***

In English on Friday, Sam is standing at his desk with a book, smiling like he can't wait to begin. "We'll be studying a very different sort of heroine," he says. "Miss Janie Crawford in Zora Neale Hurston's groundbreaking novel *Their Eyes Were Watching God*." Sam holds up the book like he's holding up a trophy. "This is a classic that should be as familiar to you as *The Wizard of Oz*. I'd like you to read it over the weekend and come in with three talking points on Monday."

"Monday," Tina says. "How many pages is it?"

Sam opens to the back of the book. "About two hundred."

"Two hundred," Ruby says. "You've got to be kidding me."

"No," Sam says, with a kind smile. "I'm not."

"How are we going to find the time to do that?" Luke says.

"Hmmm." Sam clears his throat. "Let's see. You have the whole weekend. And it takes about an hour to read twenty-five pages. I mean really read, making notes in the margin, keeping track of the characters. So, let's see. Twenty-five pages an hour . . . two-hundred-page book. Eight hours, right?"

People groan.

"Trust me"—Sam looks around at each of us—"This book will be worth every minute you give it. Every television show you watch this weekend will fly out of your mind before your alarm rings Monday morning. But a great book like this . . ." Sam holds up his trophy again. "A great book like this leaves indelible marks."

During study hall at the end of the day I finish algebra and open up to the first page of *Their Eyes Were Watching God.*

Ships at a distance have every man's wish on board. For some they come in with the tide. For others they sail forever on the horizon, never out of sight, never landing. . . . That is the life of men.

Now, women forget all those things they don't want to remember, and remember everything they don't want to forget. The dream is the truth. Then they act and do things accordingly.

I reread these first two paragraphs and underline them. "The dream is the truth." I circle that sentence, and in the margin I write, "The spirit, the hope." I think that's what the author means. "The dream is the truth."

Sam and Mom are busy making hors d'oeuvres for the social hour when I get home from school. Grilled teriyaki chicken with fresh pineapple on tiny skewers. Spears of fresh asparagus, sliced red pepper, broccoli, chunks of warm, crusty dill bread with creamy ranch dip. We serve complimentary appetizers every evening here at Bramblebriar. On the porch in the summer. By the fireplace in the winter.

"I'm too nervous to eat dinner," I say.

"Have a sandwich at least," Sam says.

"You don't want to get light-headed on stage," Mom says.

I make a half a tuna sandwich, grab some chips and a water, and head up to my room. I look over Emily's lines again. If the director has us choose a favorite scene to read, I'm going to do the one when Emily gets to return to the living for a day. She has just died giving birth to her second child, leaving behind her beloved husband, George, and four-year-old son. One of the other dead people counsels her to choose an unimportant day to live again: "Choose the least important day in your life. It will be important enough." Emily chooses her twelfth birthday. The Stage Manager—who, Mrs. Saperstone was right, is probably the star of the play—agrees to let Emily go back to the world of the living. He says to Emily: "All right. February 11th, 1899. A Tuesday. —Do you want any special time of day?"

Emily answers: "Oh, I want the whole day."

I imagine my eyes are closed, and when I open them, there is my town. Bramble. "'There's Main Street!'" I cry out with delight. "'Oh, that's the town I knew as a little girl. And, *look*, there's the old white fence that used to be around our house. Oh, I'd forgotten that! Oh, I love it so! Are they inside?'"

I can't wait to play Emily. I know what it's like to love a town, to love your family, to be in love with a boy. . . .

Thankfully, I don't have to worry about competing with Tina for the role. She decided that *Our Town* wasn't for her after all. She said, "Well, I love how that Emily girl falls in love and gets married. That's fun. But then she dies! How sad is that? And I'm sorry, but do you really expect me to believe that dead people can talk? How creepy is that?"

Mom drives me to the theater hall in Sandwich. She shuts off the engine and looks at me. "Do you want me to come in, or should I come back later?"

I'm divided down the middle like my one-side-curly, one-side-straight hair. Half of me wants her to come, half of me wants her to go. "Thanks, Mom, but I think I'll be less nervous alone. Come back at nine, okay?"

"Okay." She touches my cheek. "Good luck, Willa. I'll be rooting for you."

Something about the way she says "I'll be rooting for you" makes me want to cry. There were so many years when I felt like my mother was not on my side, not on my team, not watching my soccer games, not rooting for me . . . I gulp back tears.

I push open the heavy wooden door of the theater hall. It smells dusty and old. A tall, thin woman in black is barking out orders: "Stage Managers, row one. Emilys, row two. Georges, row three . . ."

I see JFK in the third row. *Good.* There are about thirty or forty teenagers here for try-outs, no one else I recognize from Bramble Academy. It's a small theater, about a hundred seats or so. The crimson walls are bare except for the hurricane lamps. There is a ladder on the stage and three rows of folding chairs. Something catches my eye up above, amid the jumble of lights and dangling ropes and pulleys. A small brown bird flitting from rope to rope like an acrobat.

The barking woman must be in charge. I walk toward her, smiling. She does not smile back. She is dressed in a black turtleneck and black pants, her white hair smooth in a ponytail. No jewelry, no lipstick, no color about her of any sort. Except for her eyes, a piercing stormy-sea blue. They land on me like a lighthouse beacon. "I'm the director," she says. "Who are you?"

"Willa." I laugh nervously. "Willa Havisham."

The director stares at me for a second and then looks at her clipboard. "Wrong play," she says, and turns away.

"*What?*" I am confused. My heart starts pounding.

"No Willa Havishams in *Our Town.*"

"Wait," I say. "I'm here to try out for the part of Emily. . . ."

Just then I see Mariel Sanchez walking toward

us. She moves with the grace of a ballerina, head up, shoulders back, like she doesn't have a worry in the world.

"I'm the director," the woman in black barks at Mariel. "Who are you?"

"Emily," Mariel says, so loudly people turn to look. "I am Emily Webb."

"What's that?" the director asks, pointing to a white piece of paper like a label high on the sleeve of Mariel's shirt. There is something written on it.

"My dream," Mariel says.

The director and I lean closer to read the label. It says EMILY.

CHAPTER 15

The Real Emily

The whole world's wrong, that's what's the matter.

—*Our Town*

When that weird woman, who never even tells us her name, calls up "those auditioning for the role of Emily," I strut up on stage first, towns of butterflies in my belly and everything. I give it my best effort, but even as I speak Emily's lines, I can't get fully into the part. I keep trying to spot JFK in the audience. I worry about how good Mariel will be.

Several other girls try out after me.

Mariel Sanchez goes last.

She walks up the steps and onto the stage like she owns it. Like she is Emily. Like this is her town.

Mariel Sanchez might have been Mariel

Sanchez of the raunchy, run-down Oceanview Inn of Bramble when she walked onto that stage, but when Mariel Sanchez turns and faces the audience, she is Emily Webb of Grover's Corners, New Hampshire, May 1901:

"'Oh, Mama, just look at me one minute as though you really saw me. . . . Just for a moment now we're all together. Mama, just for a moment we're happy.'"

And as Mariel speaks, I imagine her speaking to her own mother . . . telling her to go and leave and be happy.

Mariel has me in tears. She has the whole theater in tears. We are mesmerized. Mariel is Emily. *The real Emily.*

And JFK is the perfect George Gibbs:

"'Listen, Emily . . . I think that once you've found a person that you're very fond of . . . I mean a person who's fond of you, too . . .

"'Emily, if I *do* improve and make a big change . . . would you be . . . I mean: *could* you be . . .'"

Yes, yes, yes, my heart shouts. *Yes, I will marry you.*

***

When the auditions are over, the director announces, "Well done, people. Thank you for your time. I will save you the agony of a sleepless night by posting the leads right now. Practice starts Monday, promptly at seven p.m."

She pins the list on a bulletin board. I don't even have to read it.

Mariel is first in line. "Yes!" she shouts, clasping her hands together. Then she runs to JFK, her face glowing jubilantly. "Joe, you're George," she shouts, hugging him tight.

No. I stand there watching. *No.*

It's like the time when I was six and we were at the National Seashore and I was standing in the water daydreaming about something and all of a sudden this gigantic wave knocked me over and my body was hurling, *no, no,* water filling my nose and mouth, *no,* and then my face crashed down against the gravelly sand.

"Willa," JFK says, pulling himself away from Mariel to walk toward me. He looks so sweet and handsome and sorry for me.

I can't stand him feeling sorry for me. I turn to leave.

"Willa, wait."

I run outside and down the block. I sit down on a bench, my head swirling. I look back toward the theater, hoping JFK is right behind me, but he's not.

I sit crying for what feels like hours, and finally I see him coming. I wipe my face quickly and blow my nose. He sits down. "I'm sorry you didn't get the part, Willa."

I don't answer him. I picture JFK and Mariel in the wedding scene in *Our Town*. He is watching her walk down the aisle toward him. He looks so happy and handsome in his tuxedo. She looks so happy and gorgeous in her wedding gown. I start to cry again. *Grow up, Willa. You're such a baby.*

"Willa." JFK puts his arms around me. He speaks in a soft voice. "It's just a play. There will be others. I didn't realize how much that part meant to you."

"I don't want you kissing her!" I shout with such anger it surprises me.

JFK laughs. "Whoa. Is that what you're worried about?"

"It's not funny," I say, standing up.

"Hey," he says, reaching out for my arm. "Sit down."

It's dark, but the moon is bright. JFK wipes tears from my cheeks. He puts his hand under my chin and props up my face so he can look straight into my eyes. "Listen to me," he says. "I mean it, listen. When I kiss her, it will just be acting. When I kiss *you*, it's for real." Then his sweet, warm lips are on mine, and I feel like I'm melting, melting.

I look up at the sky. "'The moonlight's so *wonderful*,'" I say, quoting one of Emily's lines. "Isn't it?"

JFK laughs. "Yeah, but that director chick's scary, isn't she?"

"Yes," I say, laughing, starting to feel better. I look at my watch. "I've got to get back, my mother will be here any minute."

"Listen," JFK says. "Don't hold this against Mare, okay? She's had a lot of hard stuff in her life. This part, this particular play, is really important to her."

"Why this play?" I feel my anger rising.

"I didn't know until now," JFK says, looking away, down the street, back toward the theatre. "She just explained it to me inside. Remember how I told you her mother ran off because she landed some big role in a play?"

"I remember."

"Well, the play was *Our Town*."

When my mother pulls up, I get in quickly, close the door and face the window.

"Willa, what's the matter?" Mom asks, all concerned.

"Nothing."

Sam is up waiting for us, all hopeful, in the kitchen. Mom shakes her head and puts her fingers to her lips like, *Don't ask.*

I walk past guests chatting in the living room, run up to my room, close the door, crash on my bed. *I hate that girl. I hate that girl. Why is she trying to ruin my life? I was supposed to be Emily. I was the perfect Emily.*

I lie in bed playing each scene over and over again in my mind. How great JFK was auditioning for George Gibbs, with that goofy baseball cap and glove. How good I felt auditioning for Emily, but even as I was up on that stage trying to be Emily, I kept thinking about JFK and Mariel. I couldn't stop being Willa long enough to be Emily. And then Mariel. How she *was* Emily. The real Emily. And then how it felt so good when JFK hugged and kissed me on the bench in the dark under that perfect moon. And then how bad it felt when he explained why "Mare" needed this part so badly.

Just before I fall asleep, I picture JFK's face. I could see in his eyes just how deeply connected he is to Mariel, to her situation, to her story. . . .

And the tears come like a sea storm. I sob like a baby, like I've already lost him.

I have JFK's picture in a locket, but Mariel "Sea Bright" has his heart.

CHAPTER 16

Mother's Day

And this is Mrs. Webb's garden.
Just like Mrs. Gibbs', only it's got a lot of sun-
flowers, too.

—*Our Town*

It's Mother's Day, and Mum is delivering the ser-
mon at BUC. We are in our usual row near the
front—me, Mom, Sam, and Nana. I'm trying to listen to Mum, but I keep thinking about Mariel
Sanchez. She's sitting back in the last row, alone.

JFK and his family are off Cape this morning,
visiting his grandmother in Boston.

"Like the great author Alice Walker explained
it," Mum says, "in search of our mother's garden,
we find our own. We need to know our mother's
story and we need to know our father's story,
because they made us and we've got their roots

and we can't grow strong if we don't know what sort of plant we are."

I look sideways at my mother's face.

"I'm not saying you have to grow the way they did," Mum says. "Each one of us branches out and moves toward the sun in our own new, crazy way. But those original roots are deep down there, whether we like them or not. And we have to dig in the muck and pluck them out and study them, see them good, as much as any person can ever truly see another, and then, and only then, can we be free to bloom."

I start thinking about my mother, Stella Clancy Havisham Gracemore. Even though we've gotten closer this year, there is still so much I don't know about her past. What was she like when she was fourteen? What did she dream about? Who were her friends? Who was her first boyfriend?

"Now, here's your assignment," Mum says with a chuckle, fanning her face and adjusting the neckline of her rainbow-colored robes. "Sure is hot in here."

The congregation laughs. Mum always ends her sermons with an assignment. Something she expects us to do between now and next Sunday.

"My mama is long since gone to the angels," Mum says, "and I know many of you have lost your mothers too. This is a hard day for us. Yes, it is. But if you're lucky enough to still have your mother here in the living, or some good woman who is just like a real mother to you, I want you to look her straight in the eye and say *thank you*."

I look at my mother. There is a tear rolling down her cheek.

"It might not be all flowers and happy feelings between you," Mum says, "but I know if you think about it long enough, you can think of at least one important thing to thank her for. Something she taught you or gave you or did for you. Got it?"

"Yes, Mum," we say.

"Good," Mum says. "Now, let's close our eyes and breathe easy for a minute and thank the other one we need to thank."

That would be God.

Mum says the only prayer you ever need is just two little words long.

Thank you.

I hear the heavy door at the back of BUC open and close. I turn around to look.

Mariel Sanchez is gone.

***

After the service Sam takes us out to Moonakis for breakfast. We like the owner, Paul. He's originally from New York City, Brooklyn. The food is great, and Paul makes every customer feel special, coming around to all the tables, shaking hands, paying compliments. Paul says people should be "aggressively friendly." I like that. Aggressively friendly.

Soon our table is laden with cheese omelets, chocolate chip pancakes, sausage and bacon, cinnamon Danish, strawberry shortcake with real whipped cream. We eat until we're stuffed like turkeys.

I give Mom *Gift from the Sea*, by Anne Morrow Lindbergh. Sam suggested it.

"Thank you." She kisses me on the cheek. "You are such a thoughtful daughter, Willa."

"You're welcome, Mom." I get this weird feeling inside. This time next year my mother will have a new daughter or son. Soon there will be another child calling my mother "Mom." I can't believe it, but I think I'm jealous.

Mom and Sam give Nana a gift certificate to Mahoney's Nursery.

"Thought you'd like to pick out some annuals, Mother," Mom says to Nana. "They've got all the geraniums in now. We'll drive you over later, if you'd like."

"That would be great, dear, thanks," Nana says. She opens my present next.

It's a small garden statue, a cherub reading a book.

Nana makes a squeaking sound. Her lips tighten. I know she's thinking about Gramp, trying not to cry.

"I'm sorry, Nana. I didn't mean to make you . . ."

"Don't be sorry, sweetheart. It's perfect." She wipes away a tear, kisses the cherub on the head, and smiles. "I bet your gramp's got all the angels reading up there. He's probably starting book clubs and making God read the classics."

Sam, Mom, and I burst out laughing. Nana laughs too. A good, hearty laugh that makes us all feel better.

When we get back to the inn, Rosie is finishing up for the day. It hits me how it's Mother's Day for her, too, and here she is working instead of home with Liliana.

"Take a quiche with you, Rosie," Mom says, "and, here, I'll pack up some fruit salad and banana nut muffins. And anything else you'd like."

Rosie's face tightens. She hangs her apron on the hook, smoothes a wrinkle in the fabric. "Thank you, Stella, but we're fine."

I think Rosie is insulted. She is a very proud person. I wish she could have an easier life. I wish she could be a millionaire chef, like that Rachael Ray girl on television. Then she could set her own hours and be home with Liliana more.

Rosie has been working hard on a recipe for the Bramblebriar signature wedding cake. So far I've taste-tested at least five that I thought were winners, but Rosie still says she can do better. She comes in early and stays late trying out various combinations of sweet ingredients. Rosie says she's close, very, very close, and that it's going to be amazing. Who knows, maybe Rosie will create the perfect wedding cake. Make her big break. Get her own TV show. Sell the recipe for a million bucks. Become famous.

It's a gorgeous, sunny day, perfect beach weather. I call Tina, but the answering machine is on. Maybe JFK is back. I pack my beach bag and bike to his house.

When I turn the corner onto his street, there

are no cars in the driveway, but someone is getting off a bike. The curly black hair is unmistakable. Mariel.

My heart starts pounding. I pull my bike over behind a huge oak tree to watch.

She has a wicker basket in her hand. *Is she bringing him a picnic?*

Mariel walks up onto the porch, rings the bell, waits a minute, looks around, rings it again, then sets the basket down in front of the door. She gets on her bike and pedals off.

I wait a few seconds, then I bike up the Kennellys' driveway. *What a nerve she has. Bringing a picnic or treats, probably homemade cookies or something, to my boyfriend. My boyfriend.* I walk up the steps toward the basket. I know it's wrong. I look behind me. No neighbors around. I have no right to snoop, but I can't resist. I need to know my competition.

There is some sort of silky green fabric in the basket, with a note on top.

Dear Mrs. Kennelly,
Thank you for letting me borrow the dress. I have never been to a dance before. That night I

felt like Cinderella. Thank you, also, for buying
the ticket. I couldn't have gone otherwise. You are
a kind and thoughtful person, and I am forever
grateful for your generosity.
Love always,
Mare
PS—Nico and Sofia are still having fun with the
green mask. Peekaboo!
PSS—Happy Mother's Day.

A rush of conflicting emotions comes over me.
Relief that the basket isn't for JFK. Jealousy that
Mariel and Mrs. Kennelly are close. Sadness for
Mariel on this holiday. How badly she must miss
her own mother. . . .

I refold the note and carefully lift the dress
from the basket. It's beautiful. Underneath there's
a pair of silver sandals and a matching pocketbook. I open the pocketbook. It's empty. I feel bad.
This is wrong. I try to refold the dress exactly like
it was.

"What are you doing?" someone calls. I swing
around.

Mariel is there on her bike, staring at me. "Get
away from that," she shouts, her face flushed with

anger. "You sneak. You spy. Stay out of my business."

Then she pedals off fast, in a flurry, before I can even speak.

CHAPTER 17

Drawing in the Sand

Just for a moment now we're all together. Mama, just for a moment we're happy. Let's look at one another.

—*Our Town*

I need a walk on the beach.

I bike to the ocean with a swirling head and heavy heart. The sun is bright, but I can't feel its warmth. I choose the lion side of the Spit.

Gusts of wind whip my hair, make my eyes water. I walk and walk and walk, and the wind, like an invisible eraser, wipes my worries away, away.

Soon I start to feel better.

At the tip of the Spit the wind picks up power.

It roars at me with a force so strong that when I turn around, I can actually lean back against it. On a calm day I would surely fall, but today the wind supports me like a cub in its mother's arms.

When I round the corner onto the bay side, I see her.

Mariel is sitting in our special spot. Mine and JFK's.

Jealousy stabs me. *Have they been here together? Did he kiss her here too?*

I stand frozen stiff on the outside, a frenzy of feelings within.

Mariel, on the other hand, is the picture of peacefulness. She sits there hugging her knees to her chest, staring out at the bay. After a while she gets up and moves to the water's edge. She squats down, scoops up a handful, looks at it.

For a long time she just looks at that little bit of sea in her hand. She touches her hand to her cheek, leaves her palm there for a moment. Then she stands, picks up a piece of driftwood, kneels in the sand, and starts to draw. *Probably writing their initials. MS & JFK. In a heart with an arrow through it.* My anger rises. I hate this girl. *Why does she have to be so mysterious and different and beautiful?*

When Mariel's done writing, she flings the stick onto the dune and walks off up the beach. I wait a moment and then go to see what she wrote.

THANK YOU, MAMA.

     I LOVE YOU,

        MARE

My heart clenches. I run to catch up with her. "Mariel . . ."

At first she doesn't hear me. "Mariel . . ."

Finally she turns around. She stares at me with cold eyes.

"I'm sorry," I say, nervous and loud. "I had no right to look in the basket you left at Joseph's house."

"That's right, you didn't."

"I was wrong and—"

"It's over now," Mariel says. "You worry too much, Willa Havisham."

How does she know I worry so much? We've just barely met. . . .

"I am sorry you did not get the part," Mariel says. "But it was my dream."

My dream. That night at auditions, when the

director asked what was on her sleeve, Mariel said, "My dream."

"That was brave of you," I say. "To walk in there with 'Emily' on your sleeve."

"Not brave," Mariel says, staring me straight in the eyes. "Smart."

"What?"

"People should do that."

"Do what?"

"Wear their dreams on their sleeves."

When she says this, I get this flash of light in my head, like this is something important. "What do you mean?" I say.

"People should wear their dreams on their sleeves. So they won't forget them. And so the others can help."

"The others?" I look at her, confused but intrigued.

Mariel laughs. "They are all around us. And we need them, Willa Havisham."

"Why?"

Mariel laughs again. "To help make our dreams come true, of course." Then she turns and walks off up the beach.

"Wait," I say.

"No," she calls back. "I am late."

I start to follow, but she picks up her pace, first a quick walk, then a run.

I let her go. I sit down on the sand. I look out at the water.

Mariel is fascinating. No wonder JFK is intrigued. No wonder he likes her. How can I compete with that? I picture JFK and Mariel together at the Valentine's dance, walking together out on the Spit. . . .

I get back on my bike, take the route through town. I poke my head in the door at Sweet Bramble Books just in time to hear Nana laughing at a joke with her friend Dottie. Nana is holding her stomach, wiping tears from her eyes. "Oh, that's a good one, Dot," Nana says. "Come on in, Willa."

"No, Nana. I can't. Just wanted to say hi."

Main Street is busy today. The tables outside of Bloomin' Jean's are full of smiling faces. There's a nicely dressed family coming out of Lauren's restaurant, a happy mother in the center, basking in the attention of her special holiday.

Sulamina Mum and Riley are sitting on a bench

outside of BUC. When they see me, they wave. Riley says something to Mum and then heads off down the street.

"Willa," Mum calls. She seems excited about something, so I put a smile on my face, decide not to talk about Mariel.

"Walk with me a bit, will you," Mum says.

She unlatches the gate, and we enter the garden at the side of Bramble United Community. "The daffodils are done, but look at those hydrangeas," Mum says, pointing. "Pretty soon they'll be competing with your eyes for the prettiest blue in Bramble." I laugh and Mum does too. "And then the daisies and dahlias will start dancing, and soon after the Susans and sunflowers. . . ." Mum stops walking and looks at me. "Willa, honey, I have something to tell you."

My heart starts pounding. This can't be good.

"God knows this is hard to say, and you may feel really sad at first, but I hope you can find a way to be happy for me."

My ears close like daylilies at dusk. I don't want to hear what I know is coming.

"Riley and I are getting married and . . ." Mum's voice breaks. "I am finally going home."

Mum looks so happy. Somehow I manage to smile. I hug her and tell her how glad I am for her and Riley. Then I say I'm late for dinner. I bike home in a daze.

Mum can't go. I need her. I love her.

As soon as I reach the inn, I go to find my mother. She is lying out on the back terrace on a lounge chair. Her eyes are closed. With her silky black hair and rosy cheeks, she looks like Sleeping Beauty.

I smile thinking about how she hated all that princess stuff when I was little. She'd roll her eyes at commercials for expensive dolls and makeup kits. She refused to let me help her with the weddings. She was afraid I would get all foggy-brained and lose focus on school. "I don't want you to be one of those girls who sits around painting her nails, waiting for Prince Charming to rescue her," she'd say. "You are smart and strong, Willa Havisham, and you can take care of yourself."

I don't feel smart or strong at the moment.

My mother opens her eyes and yawns.

For a few seconds she just stares at me. Then she smiles and beckons. "Come here, baby."

And something about the way my mother says "baby" makes me start to bawl like one. I collapse into the wicker chair with her, thinking about JFK and Mariel and Mum.

My mother strokes my hair and whispers, "It's okay. Whatever it is. We'll work it out."

And as awful as I feel, I pretend that she is right.

"Thanks, Mom. I love you."

"I love you, too, baby. Love you, too."

CHAPTER 18

Three Favors for Mum

I'm celebrating because I've got a friend who tells me all the things that ought to be told me.

—*Our Town*

The whole town of Bramble was very generous with books for our Community Service project. The gymnasium at Bramble Academy is over-flowing with boxes.

The freshman class meets after school to sort the books into categories. I mark the four corners of the room. "Picture books that way. Early readers, like Dr. Seuss and the Frog and Toad books, that way. Middle readers, say fourth through eighth grades, in that corner. Teenage stuff over there. If you have any questions, ask me or Sam or Mrs. Saperstone."

A well-worn copy of *Make Way for Ducklings* catches my eye. I used to love that book. I think about the baby on the way. How much fun it will be reading to a little one.

"Will the hours we put in count toward next year?" Ruby asks in a huff. "Because we're already done for this year."

Sam looks at me and winks. I want to say, "Ruby, we're never done," but I just say, "I'll check into that."

At dinner Mom says, "This weekend is Memorial Day. Let's kick off the summer with a barbecue. Willa, why don't you invite Joseph and his family, too. I'd like to get to know the Kennellys better. And Tina, Ruby . . . whoever you want from school. Just tell everyone to bring a salad or dessert to share. We'll handle the grill."

I remember another Memorial Day picnic. Sam had just moved into town, and I invited him over for a barbecue. At first my mother got mad, but then she agreed.

"I'll set up badminton," Sam says, "and croquet, horseshoes, bocce."

"If it's warm enough, we could even swim in the pond," Mom says.

"Might be a good time to test out the *ganola* boats," I say, and we laugh. Mom and I have been working hard on Suzy-Jube's wedding. The menu is set, the flowers, the music . . . an orchestra, a DJ, and Shirley Happyfeet—we've got tango to two-step covered . . . the Blazers' family minister is handling the ceremony, and drumroll, please, the Bramblebriar signature wedding cake will make its grand debut. All I can tell you is that Rosie has created the most mouthwatering, wonderful wedding cake confection the world has ever known. Oh, and I'll let you in on a surprise. I will be adding twelve secret ingredients to our signature cake.

Bet you can't guess what they are.

When I call to invite Tina to the Memorial Day picnic, she asks if she can bring Jessie. "Sure," I say, "the more the merrier."

My fingers fumble as I dial JFK's phone number.

When his mother answers, I have this sudden urge to hang up the receiver, but I don't. "Hi, Mrs. Kennelly, this is Willa Havisham. Is Joseph there?"

Mrs. Kennelly laughs. "No need to use last names, Willa. I think I should know my son's girl-friend's name."

Girlfriend? Whoopee! I giggle. "Oh, sorry."

"Joseph's at baseball practice right now, and then he's got play practice, but I can have him call when he gets home."

Our Town. How could I forget?

"Sure, thanks. Actually, I was calling to invite your family to a Memorial Day barbecue on Saturday. Here at the inn at three p.m."

"That sounds great, thanks. We'll bring potato salad and brownies."

The next day after school I stop by Mum's. She is watering a plant in a clay pot on the porch. "What's that?" I ask.

"A sorry little tomato plant," Mum says, touch-ing a yellowy green leave. "Oh . . . when Riley and I go home, I can't wait to buy a little house of my own with flowers out front and vegetables out back. I'm tired of living in other people's places. All my life I've wanted a piece of earth to call my own. Not much. Just a patch that was mine."

All this time I thought Mum owned this house.

She works so hard, does such important work. It doesn't seem right that she can't afford her own house.

"I have three favors to ask you, Willa. So sit a spell, if you can."

"*Three* favors?"

"Yep. Sit there and I'll get us some iced tea. Just brewed it fresh this morning."

Mum hands me a glass. I take a sip. "*Mmmm.* It's so sweet and fruity. I've never tasted iced tea like this before."

"That's 'cause you never spent a summer in the South," Mum says. "One way or the other, we find a way to put peach into everything." She laughs and I do too.

"Okay," Mum says. "Favor number one. Riley and I want to get married at Bramblebriar, and we'd like you to plan it."

"Oh, Mum, of course. I'd be honored."

"Good. And speaking of honors, that's favor number two. I'd like you to be my maid of honor."

My heart quickens, my nose tickles, and tears well up in my eyes. "Oh, Mum." I reach toward her. Hugging Mum is like hugging a pillow. A big, soft, lumpy pillow that smells like baby powder. "I would love to. Thank you for asking me. Have you and Riley set a date yet?"

"Yes, we have. Sunday, June eleventh."

Oh, no. The day after Suzy-Jube's wedding. "Is that date set in stone?"

"Yes, honey, it is. I always say, when it's time to move on, say your good-byes and go. No sense loading a bucket full of tears. Riley's already ordered the U-Haul van. We'll be leaving Bramble bright and early June twelfth, with my few sorry boxes of belongings and a whole big truck full of the books you collected."

"But Mum, why do you have to go so soon? Can't you . . ." I scrunch my lips tight to keep from crying. I try to be brave.

"Willa, honey." She touches my arm gently. "Believe me, my heart's breaking too. But I lost this man once before, and God knows, I ain't going to lose him again."

I sip my peach tea and zip my lips. *Grow up, Willa. You want Mum to be happy, don't you? She would want you to be happy.* "Hey, Mum, I almost forgot. We're having a picnic on Saturday and we want you and Riley to come."

"Wouldn't miss it for the world," Mum says.

"Good," I say, getting up to leave. "Mom said to bring a salad or dessert."

"Tell Stella I'll bring peach pie."

"Sounds good, Mum. I'll see you later. Oh, wait. You said *three* favors."

"That's right. Okay. Now, this may be the hardest." Mum locks her eyes with mine. "Remember when you were new in Bramble and you were having troubles with your mother and I knew you had a heart of gold and I tried to be your friend?"

"Sure, Mum, I remember."

"Good. 'Cause there's a new girl in town with a mighty good heart who is carrying a heavy sack of sorrow, and I think she could use a friend like you."

I don't even need to hear the name. Mum's talking about Mariel.

CHAPTER 19

The Lead

Life's awful funny!

—*Our Town*

I'm lying on my bed flipping through *My Ántonia*, by Willa Cather. *Willa.* Just like me. When I was younger, my mother insisted on calling me Willafred. That's the name she got from combining my birth father's first and middle names, William and Frederick. Thankfully, everyone calls me Willa. Willa, like a willow tree. So much nicer than Willafred, don't you think?

I remember one rainy afternoon Gramp Tweed and I were sitting in the bookstore on the old couch with our feet propped up, drinking our signature lemon tea. He said, "You have a literary namesake, you know. Willa Cather. One of the bright lights." He looked at me and winked. "And

I suspect that one day students of American liter-ature will be talking about 'the two Willas.'"
Gramp always said he thought I'd be a writer.

I swallow back tears. I close my eyes. *I love you, Gramp. I miss you.*

Then I remember what Nana said at the restau-rant on Mother's Day.

So, what are you and God reading this week, Gramp? I laugh and feel better.

I flip through chapter 1 of *My Ántonia* to see what I marked the first time I read it. If I own a book—not borrowed from the library but it's mine—I always read with a pen in my hand. That way I can circle the parts I like and write notes to myself in the margin, little stars and smiley faces, question marks, how something rings true for me.

"That is happiness; to be dissolved into some-thing complete and great."

I circled that line the first time. Now I make stars around it.

". . . dissolved into something complete and great."

That's how I sometimes feel when I'm reading.

That's how I sometimes feel when I'm writing. Fingers flying across the page, words flowing fast as a waterfall. It's like in that movie, *Chariots of Fire,* when the man says he feels God when he is running. I understand that. I feel God when I am writing.

"That is happiness; to be dissolved into something complete and great."

I read somewhere that this quote is inscribed on Willa Cather's gravestone in Jaffrey Center, New Hampshire. I'd like to visit there someday. Jaffrey Center, New Hampshire. Grover's Corners, New Hampshire.

Our Town.

I should have gotten the part of Emily.

"Willa." Sam is knocking on my bedroom door. I open it. He has a strange look on his face. "There's a woman downstairs who wants to speak with you. I asked her name, and all she said was 'the director.'"

My heart leaps. *Yes.* Thank you. Talk about answering prayers. Finally that dreary woman came to her senses and realized what an awful mistake she made and that I, of course, am the perfect Emily. I run down the stairs.

The director is sitting by the fireplace. "Miss Havisham," she says, coming to shake my hand, her long, lean arm outstretched. She is wearing a black blouse, long black skirt, and shawl. "Thank you for seeing me."

"Sure." My heart is racing. "Can I get you something? Coffee? Water?"

She shakes her head no. "I have an offer for you," she says, "an invitation."

My head is pounding. "Yes?" I say, trying to appear calm, trying not to sound too desperate, but unable to stop the huge smile springing out across my face.

"I realize it is the proverbial eleventh hour, but I hope you will consider joining our humble troupe in the distinguished role of . . ." She pauses, probably for the dramatic effect.

Emily, Emily. "Yes?"

"Stage Manager." She says this as if it is the most exciting news in the world.

"What?" A pin pops my smiley-face balloon and all of the air whooshes out.

"Yes," the director says, clearly pleased with herself. "I realize this must come as a shock to you. I actually had cast you in that role in my mind from the start, but you read for the part of Emily. And so I cast my second choice, young

Gerald from Cotuit, but alas, young Gerald has had a medical emergency and cannot fulfill his obligation. I need a Stage Manager. Fast. Someone who can learn the lines in a matter of weeks. We open June twenty-first."

"But I tried out for Emily," I say quietly. *Don't cry, Willa, be strong. Don't embarrass yourself in front of this cold, cruel, black-hearted . . . woman.*

The director focuses her lighthouse rays on me. "You see the world through a poet's eyes, all the colors, all the nuances. Emily is not so introspective. Emily doesn't think so much—she just does."

I let that sink in a bit. "But that's the best part. Emily is—"

"You may not realize this, Miss Havisham," the director interrupts, raising her hand in the air as if to say *Cut*. "But I was watching you carefully the night of auditions. I studied each potential player as she or he entered the theater hall. What I noticed about you was how you took it all in—the room, the people, the ripped curtain, the overturned coffee cup, the kid picking his nose by the ticket booth, even that tiny sparrow flitting from rope to rope above us . . . you were awake and aware of it all. That is the role of the Stage

Manager in Wilder's town. The Stage Manager is the omniscient, the all-seeing eye. *Our Town,* metaphor for every town, everywhere, every age, begins and ends with the Stage Manager. Only this one character sees the past, present, and future. Only this one knows the stories of all the others on the stage and off of the stage, how all the threads are connected, how each connects to the web, and how it all so miraculously, so majestically, *makes sense.* I am asking you to play the lead, Miss Havisham. Will you accept?"

The lead? I feel a strange rush of emotion. *Me?*

"What worries you?" the director asks, cocking her head to the side, studying me.

"I don't know if I can. . . ."

"I would not ask if I were not certain," the director says. "I believe you have the mind, more importantly, the heart."

Then she smiles.

And perhaps because it is the first time I have ever seen the director smile, it is especially moving. All of a sudden I feel confident. "All right," I say. "I accept."

"Good." She stands abruptly, turns to leave. "Practice tomorrow, seven p.m."

***

I bike straight to JFK's house. He answers the door. I tell him my news.

"Awesome," he says. "That's great." He hugs me.

"Come on in," he says. "My parents will be back soon."

He grabs two bottles of water from the fridge and hands me one. We go downstairs. "Want to play bumper pool?" he says.

I've played only once or twice before, but I'm actually pretty good. JFK seems surprised. He wins. "How about Ping-Pong?" he says.

"Sure."

It's close, but I beat him.

"Whoa," JFK says. "Where'd you learn to play like that?"

"Oh, I don't know," I say, smiling coyly. "One of my other boyfriends taught me a few tricks. I can't remember who. . . ."

"Come here," he says, laughing, lunging toward me.

I giggle and run. He chases me around the Ping-Pong table. We're both pretty fast. He tags me and tackles me down on the couch. We crack up laughing. My heart is pounding, I'm all out of breath.

"There better not be any other boyfriends," he says sweetly.

He kisses me. He smells so good.

I think Ping-Pong's my new favorite sport.

CHAPTER 20

Summer on Old Cape Cod

*I declare, you got to speak to George. Seems like
something's come over him lately. . . .
. . . All he thinks about is that baseball.*

—*Our Town*

Saturday is sunny and warm, perfect for the
first picnic of summer.

Sam is marinating chicken and ribs in his
famous, secret-recipe honey barbecue sauce.
When Sam fires up the grill later today and that
delicious aroma wafts through the air, every
mouth in Bramble will be watering, wishing it
could come to the party.

Unfortunately, JFK and his family aren't coming. A rained-out baseball game got rescheduled

for this afternoon, and the field is way out in Wellfleet.

"You know Cape boys and their baseball," Mrs. Kennelly said when she called.

Well, I didn't, but I do now. Baseball, baseball, baseball. It seems like JFK has a game or a practice, or a game and a practice, every single day.

Mom and Sam and I head out to the picnic tables.

My friends from school start showing up. Tina and Jessie Shefali. Luke and Emily. Alexa, Gus, and Ruby and Chris Ruggiero. Finally JFK is off of Ruby's radar screen.

"Volleyball," Luke shouts, and we head over to the net.

As we're finishing our game, Nana arrives in a loopy straw hat, carrying cellophane bags of penny candy for all my friends.

"I love you, Nana," Tina says, giving my grandmother a kiss on the cheek.

"I love you, too, sweetie," Nana says.

Nana is a big, big hit with my friends.

"Your mother looks so happy today," Tina says. "She's got that dreamy look. On *Forever Young* they call it the mommy glow. It's so *in* to be pregnant right now. No more mousy maternity clothes. It's all about showing off your baby bump."

"Baby bump?" I say. *Forever Young* is Tina's favorite soap opera. It's one of the many things we don't have in common. It's a wonder we are best friends.

Mrs. Saperstone comes next, pulling a red wagon behind her. "I made a batch of gazpacho," she says. "I hope that was okay?"

"Okay?" Sam says. "It's wonderful. My favorite. Thank you."

"And this is for you, Willa," Mrs. Saperstone says, handing me a book. "You enjoyed *Wuthering Heights* so much, I thought this might strike your fancy."

"Thanks, Mrs. S."

Rebecca, by Daphne du Maurier. I open the book and read the first line: "Last night I dreamt I went to Manderley again." *Nice.* "First things first," I say when it comes to books. I want that first line to hook me and reel me in. This one does. "Last night I dreamt I went to Manderley again." *Nice.*

Sulamina Mum and Riley come, each carrying a pie.

"Sorry we're late," Mum says. "Just took these out of the oven."

"*Mmmm*, smells so good," my mother says, setting the pies down. "I may keep one for myself." She laughs. "And *congratulations* on your engagement, Sulamina!"

"Thank you," Mum says. "And thank you for letting us have the reception here, Stella. Willa said you already have another wedding scheduled the day before."

"No problem," my mother says. "After all you've done for me and Willa, it will be our absolute pleasure."

Riley gives Mum a big kiss. "Am I the luckiest man in the world or what?"

"I might have to challenge you on that," Sam says, putting his arm around my mother's waist. My mother smiles. I think back to that other Memorial Day picnic, when my mother was so uptight, too afraid yet to let Sam into her life, into our lives. . . .

I photograph this moment in my mind. All the happy faces. My family and our friends laughing, talking, playing croquet and horseshoes . . . the tables heavy with food . . . puffy blue hydrangeas and red rambling roses climbing the fence. It's like some Norman Rockwell painting. *Summer on Old Cape Cod*, I'd call it. What do you think, Norman?

Thank you, my heart prays. *Thank you*.

Sulamina Mum is watching me with a quizzical expression on her face.

"What?" I say.

Mum looks around. "I was just thinking how nice it is we're all here together on this sunny summer day. Especially you teenagers. Fine young people. All of you."

Mum stares into my eyes.

I know it's one of those moments when Mum wants me to understand something, but she's in no hurry, she'll wait as long as it takes for me to figure it out myself. "What?" I say again. My friends are running toward the pond, laughing.

"Come on, Willa," Tina shouts over, "let's take out a boat."

"Be right there." I turn back to Mum. "Give me a hint at least."

"Plenty of food to go around. What's one more friend at the table, right?"

Slowly it dawns on me. *Mariel*. "Are we talking about favor number three?"

Mum's face lights up with a smile. "That's my girl," she says.

Well, at least JFK isn't at the picnic, I think as I bike to Mariel Sanchez's house. The waste treatment plant smells like dead fish decaying on the beach. If it smells this bad at the start of summer, I wonder what it's like in August.

Someone has stuck a row of tiny American flags under the dirty Oceanview Inn sign. It's the only indication of a holiday. The place is eerily quiet except for the droning of an air conditioner in the window of the office. I think of the beautiful house I live in. How lucky I am. I remember the letter I wrote to the paper about Come Home Cape Cod. I hope they get the money to build lots of houses for people.

As I get closer and pass by rooms, I hear all the television sets, different channels, a baby crying, a man shouting angrily in a language I don't know, every window cranked in hopes of a breeze.

When I knock on number 6, a man says, "Come in." My stomach is flipping like a fish on a hook. Then, even before I can turn the knob, the door opens.

Mariel stares at me with wide eyes. She has a book in her hand.

"I know," I say, smiling awkwardly. "You're probably wondering what I'm doing here."

"Invite your friend in," Mr. Sanchez says, wheeling toward me, nodding. The microwave beeps, and he wheels back around to it, opens the door, takes out a plate of food. "Nico, Sofia," he says, "wash your hands."

I hear giggling, and then the twins poke their heads out from underneath the bed. "Boo!" they shout, thrusting chocolate-coated palms in the air toward me.

"Oooh, you scared me," I say, playing along.

"I told you, no candy before dinner," Mariel says.

Nico and Sofia hug Mariel the way little kids hug their mother when a stranger is near.

"We're having a barbecue at my house," I say, "and Sulamina Mum is there and Mrs. Saperstone."

"Oh, I see," Mariel says, "they told you to invite—"

"No," I say. "I came to tell you that I'm going to be in *Our Town* after all. The Stage Manager. I thought maybe you could fill me in on what I've missed at practices."

"Truly?" Mariel says.

"Truly," I say. "Do you have a bike? If we hurry, we'll be just in time for my father's famous barbecued chicken."

"Of course you will go," Mr. Sanchez says. He smiles, shooing his daughter away. "Go, Mariel, go enjoy."

We bike alongside each other. The rim on the front tire of Mariel's bike is green. The rim on the back is orange.

"Mrs. Saperstone told me how you saved the Bramble Library," she says.

We start talking about books. Mariel loved *Their Eyes Were Watching God* too. Right now she's reading *The Scarlet Letter*, by Nathaniel Hawthorne. I make a mental note to put that on my summer list. Mariel says she and her father plan her lessons in the morning before he leaves for work. Mrs. Santiago, the lady in number 7, watches Nico and Sofia when Mariel needs to run errands or go to the library.

"No wonder you swim so early in the morning,"

I say. "It sounds like that's the only time you have to yourself."

"It is okay," Mariel says quickly. "In a family everybody has to do their part."

Before I know it, we're back at the inn, walking toward the picnic tables, laughing about the director.

"What's with all the black?" Mariel says, giggling.

"I know," I say. "And what the heck is her name, anyway?"

And then Tina and Ruby are standing there, staring at us.

"We wondered where you went, Willa," Tina says, not smiling.

Ruby is looking down at Mariel's old sneakers.

I introduce Mariel to my friends, painfully aware of how Tina and Ruby are sizing up Mariel's clothing. Green shorts, too long for the style this summer, pink T-shirt with chocolate fingerprints on the front.

Mariel follows their gaze. She swipes at the chocolate, making the stains worse. "I should have changed," she says.

I feel my face getting hot. I look at Tina and Ruby with their perfect clothes, perfect hair, perfect summer-pink pedicures. "Come on, Mare, I've got a shirt you can borrow."

When we walk inside the inn, Mariel says, "Your home is beautiful."

As we head upstairs, I realize Mariel is more my mother's size. I fish a few shirts out of my mother's drawer. Mariel chooses a plain white pocket tee. My mother has a dozen of them. I start to say, "Don't worry about returning it," but then I remember how insulted Rosie was on Mother's Day, and I decide Mariel is probably proud too.

In my room Mariel moves to my bookcase like metal to a magnet. "Wow," she says, running her hand along the spines, just the way I would if I had just seen all these books. She tilts her head to read the titles. "Yes." She nods, smiling. "Yes," clearly recognizing some favorites of her own. "These are all yours?" she says. "You own them?"

"Yes."

Mariel looks at me. "You are lucky."

I smile and nod. "I know. Listen, anytime you want to borrow—"

"Thank you," Mariel says, "but the library serves me fine."

I think how sad it is that Mariel doesn't own the

books she reads. It must be hard for someone who loves books so much not to be able to write notes in the margin, circle lines she loves, draw little smiley faces and stars next to her favorite passages. . . .

The first picnic of the summer is a smashing success. After dark we roast marshmallows in the old stone fireplace. "Look," Mariel says, pointing, "a firefly." Tina squints her eyes at Mariel, not smiling, but my other friends seem to like her okay.

Nana offers to put Mariel's bike in her station wagon and give her a lift home. "Thank you for inviting me, Willa," Mariel says. "I had a wonderful time."

"She's nice," I write in my journal later.

But when I close my eyes to sleep, I picture Mariel hugging JFK. I picture them kissing during the wedding scene of *Our Town*, and I am wide awake again.

Why did I invite her to my house? Introduce her to my friends?

What was I thinking of?

CHAPTER 21

Cheesecakes

EMILY: *Do any human beings ever realize life while they live it?—every, every minute?*
STAGE MANAGER: *. . . The saints and poets, maybe— they do some.*

—*Our Town*

Sam is leaning against his desk leafing through a well-worn book when we file in to English class. It's June, and I feel that old familiar seesaw inside. Worried about finals, excited about vacation, worried about finals, excited about vacation. And this June I've also got two weddings and *Our Town* to think about too.

I look back at JFK. He winks at me and smiles.

We'll have the whole summer together. Just the two of us. Well, as soon as baseball is over, that is.

When we're settled at our desks, Sam adjusts

his glasses and reads aloud:

> *"A child said What is the grass? fetching it to me with*
> *full hands;*
> *How could I answer the child? I do not know what it is*
> *any more than he.*
> *I guess it must be the flag of my disposition, out of hope-*
> *ful green stuff woven."*

My mind wanders, wondering about the little son Sam lost years ago. Did he have Sam's eyes? That Sam-smile that melts your heart?

"Walt Whitman's *Leaves of Grass*," Sam says. "Every summer I return to Whitman's grass and *Walden's* pond. And each summer I find new treasures."

Sam flips through *Leaves of Grass*. I know he's looking for some passage he has circled. It was Sam who taught me always to read a book with a pen in my hand.

Sam finds what he's looking for and continues:

> *"I celebrate myself, and sing myself,*
>
> *. . . .*
>
> *I loafe and invite my soul,*

I lean and loafe at my ease observing a spear of summer
grass."

I look around the room. All eyes are on Sam. It is impossible to be bored or sleepy or distracted when someone is so passionately sharing his joy.

"This is the grass that grows wherever the land is and the
water is,
This is the common air that bathes the globe.

"'Bathes the globe,'" Sam repeats. "And this," Sam says, leaning forward, "this takes my breath away. . . ."

"I believe a leaf of grass is no less than the journey-work
of the stars."

I write that in my notebook. "The journey-work of the stars."

I think of stars as stationary. I know people see them fall, but I have never seen one move. I can't wait to buy *Leaves of Grass* so I can write in it, make it my own.

Sam picks up another book from his desk.

There's a frayed string hanging from the spine. Another well-worn, well-loved book. "My other summer friend," Sam says.

He is silent for a few seconds. We watch him, waiting.

"Thoreau's *Walden*," he says, tapping the book's cover like he's applauding it, now gently stroking it like a beloved pet. "I once thought of following in Thoreau's footsteps, going off and living alone in the woods to search my soul. I was burned out from teaching in an overcrowded school. My wife and son had died in a car crash the year before . . ."

The new girl, Shefali, gasps. She didn't know that about Sam.

". . . and I was desperate to find some meaning in my life." Sam slides his reading glasses back up the bridge of his nose. He looks so handsome and distinguished. I look around the room. *Do you all realize this man is my father?*

Sam reads aloud from *Walden*:

"I went to the woods because I wished to live deliberately, to front only the essential facts of life, and see if I could not learn what it had to teach, and not, when I came to die, discover that I had not lived."

"That's depressing," Tina says.

I turn to her like she's crazy. *That's fascinating,* I think. I wonder if Sam still wishes he could go off and search his soul, alone. I think of Mariel's mother going off in search of her dream. I think how Mariel would love this class. I look at Tina. She's looking at Ruby. They roll their eyes.

"Don't these writers make you want to start your summer reading today?" Sam says.

There are a few snickers throughout the room. *Yes,* I think. *Yes.*

"In just a few weeks," Sam says, "you lucky people will have a whole long, glorious summer to lounge on the grass, soaking in books."

"I'll be soaking in the sun," Ruby says, and people laugh.

"That's right," Sam says, "nothing better than reading on the beach."

The bell rings, and we gather up to go.

"Don't forget. Our final text. *To Kill a Mockingbird.* Next week."

It's late when I get home from practice. I love being the Stage Manager. Mrs. Saperstone was right. It's the best character. I've got some of the greatest lines: "Yes, it's clearing up. There are the stars—doing their old, old crisscross journeys in the sky."

There's that journey theme again. What did Whitman say? "The journey-work of the stars." Then Wilder's "crisscross journeys in the sky." I love those lines. Poetry.

I remember the summer we first moved here to Bramble and I spotted that man next door putting poetry on the little billboard on his front lawn. I called him the Poet before I learned his real name.

His name was Sam—Sam Gracemore.

Soon his name will be "Dad."

I can't find Sam in the inn. "I think he's outside," Mom says.

The herb garden smells spicy. Dill, rosemary, thyme. The vegetable garden is thriving too. Sam is proud of his three types of lettuce, four kinds of peppers, this year.

It's dark back here, but the moon is bright. Sam is sitting on the stone bench in the center of the labyrinth. His eyes are closed. He looks peaceful.

Sam walks the labyrinth only early in the morning or late when the guests have retired for the night. He designed and planted this amazing maze himself. It's a circle within a circle within a circle. The narrow pathway is bordered on both sides by perennial flowers and shrubs. You enter and follow the outer rim, then curve inward, then outward, then inward again, weaving in closer, than farther away, then toward the center, then out to the border, as you make your way to the resting bench in the middle. The bench is the bull's-eye. I think of it as God's eye. Sam's sacred place.

I stand here staring at this good, good man who is now my father.

My birth father, William Frederick Havisham, was a man of big, brash, wild ideas. His crazy scheme to whisk my mother off on their honeymoon in a hot-air balloon ended in a tragedy. It took my mother more than a decade to overcome the shock and pain of his death. She was frozen like a statue with grief, too afraid or angry to love again.

Sam is a different sort of man. This labyrinth is his Walden Pond, his wild hot-air balloon. Sam's dream is rooted strong in the earth. He won't float away from us.

I think about running through the labyrinth right now and giving Sam his Father's Day present early: "Happy Father's Day, Dad."

I have practiced that moment over and over in my mind.

But no, I'll wait. I won't spoil the surprise.

Tina calls to talk about Suzanna Jubilee's wedding again.

The Blazers will descend on Bramble next Friday for the rehearsal dinner, sixteen brides-maids and ushers in tow. Tina and Ruby are planning on sneaking in.

"Willa, think about it," Tina says. "If those sixteen bridesmaids are beauty pageant winners, those ushers will be *cheesecakes*."

"Don't you mean 'beefcakes'?" I say.

"Cheesecakes, beefcakes, wedding cakes. Who the cake cares, Willa? You worry about the words, all I want to do is feast my eyes on sixteen gorgeous, hunky guys."

"But what about Jessie?" I ask. "Aren't you still going out?"

"What about him?" Tina says. "You know he's my love muffin. But a girl can still check out the bakery, right? Nothing wrong with looking at the cheesecakes."

CHAPTER 22

Twelve Secret Ingredients

Most everybody's asleep in Grover's Corners.
There are a few lights on: Shorty Hawkins, down
at the depot, has just watched the Albany train
go by.

—*Our Town*

It's the night before Suzanna Jubilee's wedding
and everyone is asleep. I tiptoe down to the
kitchen with a certain faded white satin satchel.
I'm on a secret mission. It's time to add twelve
secret ingredients to the wedding cake. The delec-
tably delicious, melt-in-your-mouth-like-taffy,
decadently rich, and, as Tina would say, *absolutely-
to-die-for* Bramblebriar signature wedding cake
that Chef Rosie has so brilliantly concocted.

Mom doesn't know about the secret ingredients. Suzanna, either. Everyone will be surprised.

Life can be boring without surprises, don't you think?

You may know that when Mom was a wedding planner, I used to add a secret ingredient to her perfect wedding plans. My intentions were good when I sewed a cherry pit into the hem of each Weddings by Havisham bridal gown on the night before a wedding. It was my way of planting a bit of love, a metaphorical seed of good luck for the happy marriage that would hopefully bloom the day after the fancy wedding. But alas, my little tradition caused a calamity of catastrophic proportions and ruined the most famous wedding my mother ever planned.

I planted my last cherry pit when Mom and Sam got married and we moved here, into the Bramblebriar Inn. There's a little cherry tree growing out front to remind me.

I'm older and wiser now. Mom is too. I'm happy she's getting back into the wedding-planning business. And now that she's letting me be her partner, I am not going to do anything to screw this up.

But I do want to add something new, something good.

In the kitchen I turn on the lights, open the pastry refrigerator, and carefully lift out Rosie's masterpiece.

Following my instructions, Rosie left a hollow space—"a wishing well," as I called it—on the top tier of the cake so that I could "add the magic," as Rosie called it.

I open the satchel and shake the twelve silver charms onto the counter. Each charm is wrapped in plastic, with long satin ribbons of different colors attached.

I line the charms up in order.

A book for *B*.

A rose for *R*.

An angel for *A*.

A mirror for *M*.

A beach dune for *B*.

A labyrinth for *L*.

An envelope for *E*.

A butterfly for *B*.

A ring for *R*.

An inkwell for *I*.

An anchor for *A*.

A rainbow for *R*.

"Bramblebriar."

I actually have Tina to thank for the idea. When she told me to go online and research currently popular wedding trends so I wouldn't plan anything embarrassingly old-fashioned, I came across a new-old wedding custom so charming and romantic I knew immediately that it was perfect for us.

It was easy to find most of the charms. The labyrinth took a bit more time. So appropriate, don't you think? Labyrinths do take time. Mr. Wickstrom at the jewelry store came through for me. He's such a nice man. I'm thinking of playing cupid for him and Mrs. Saperstone. I think they'd make a good couple.

I lift the crystal bride-and-groom centerpiece from the top of the cake and set it on the counter. I carefully place each of the charms into the wishing well, one at a time, smiling as I think about what each one means to me, then I gently drape the shiny ribbons down over the tiers of the cake like a rainbow waterfall and put the bride and groom back on top.

Tomorrow at the reception I will instruct the

wedding guests to look under their dinner plates. Twelve pennies will be randomly placed at tables throughout the room. Those who find a penny will get to pull a ribbon from the wishing well before Suzy and Simon cut the cake.

There are many versions of this tradition, and the charms usually come with a meaning attached. A clover for luck. A ring says you'll marry soon. But I decided to let each person assign his or her own meaning to the charm. Everyone has different hopes and dreams. I think the charms will have more power, more magic, if people decide what the charms mean to them.

I stand back and smile at the cake.

I hope Suzanna will be pleased

I hope my mother will be proud.

Hurrying back upstairs in the dark, I nearly collide with Papa B Blazer.

"Willa!" he shouts, all flustered and disheveled. "You scared me!"

"I'm sorry, Papa B. Are you all right?"

"Oh, yes, fine as fudge. It's just that I forgot to hang the beads."

"The what?"

"The rosary beads. Mama B. says if you hang rosaries on the line the night before an important occasion, then God will sure as shootin' send you sunny weather."

"That's nice, Papa B. Good luck."

I'll have to remember to put rosaries out for Mum and Riley, too.

Just before I fall asleep, I remember something. I head back downstairs, grab a flashlight, and go out to change the Bramble Board.

SUZANNA AND SIMON:
ON THIS, YOUR WEDDING DAY,
EVERY BIRD SINGS ITS SWEETEST SONG FOR YOU,
EVERY STAR SHINES ITS BRIGHTEST LIGHT.
WE WISH YOU ALL THE HAPPINESS TWO HEARTS CAN HOLD.
YOUR FRIENDS FOREVER AT THE BRAMBLEBRIAR INN

As I walk back inside, I see the rosary beads hanging from my little cherry tree.

Life's awful funny, don't you think?

CHAPTER 23

Suzanna Jubilee's Wedding

Perfectly lovely wedding! Loveliest wedding I ever saw.

Oh, I do love a good wedding, don't you?

—Our Town

When I look out my window in the morning, the sky is so blue it doesn't seem real. It's that crayon color I picked at five to paint a perfect picture. No clouds, not even the wispy ones. The sun is casting diamonds across the pond, and a sweet breeze, like music, is rustling through the trees and over the leaves of grass.

It's the sort of wedding day every bride dreams of and every bride deserves.

My mother comes to help me get ready. "The

maid of honor deserves special pampering," she says. Our hairdresser, Jo, suggested I curl both sides of my hair today. "Be curly all over for a change." Mom gently lifts a lock of my hair and fastens it with a tiny butterfly-shaped clip. She hooks the back of my gown, a silky chiffon, the color of lemon sherbet, with a poofy skirt that will swirl when I dance.

"Yellow brings out the summer highlights in your hair," Mom says, "so pretty." She checks my face, adds a bit more eyeliner and mascara, brushes my cheeks with a bronze powder, and touches up my lipstick. "There," she says. "Beautiful."

She looks into my eyes and smiles, a sweet-sad expression on her face.

"You have your father's eyes. Sparkling like the sea on a sunny summer day."

My birth father, William Frederick Havisham. I remember she described his eyes that way in a poem I found long ago in a heart-shaped box in her closet.

"Sam has blue eyes too," I say.

"That's right," Mom says, her face brightening. She looks at the clock. "Oh, I need to get dressed myself. It's nearly showtime!"

***

The sixteen bridesmaids are gathered downstairs in the living room. Sam is out by the pond overseeing the ushers with the seating of guests. The bride and groom are safely sequestered out in their matching "ganolas" on either side of the pond, shaded from view until the wedding begins.

The beauty queens are buzzing about in a flurry, checking one another's hair and makeup, adjusting their sashes in the mirror. Suzanna generously said they could all wear their favorite pageant gowns, and so no two bridesmaids are dressed alike.

"Suzanna Jubilee is a sugarplum, a sugarcoated sugarplum," Miss Georgia-Grown 2008 gushes, adjusting the tiara nestled in a towering bouffant of tomato red hair. "Imagine, lettin' us pick our favorite pageant gowns instead of matching us up together like a string of paper dolls."

"Suzy-Jube isn't threatened by other people's beauty," Miss Whappinger Falls 2007 says, dabbing some perfume down the valley on her chest. Mom had to kick Sam under the table at the rehearsal dinner to stop him from staring at Miss Whappinger.

The grandfather clock chimes 3:00 p.m., and

Sam pops his head into the room, so handsome in his tuxedo. "The guests have all been seated."

"What a stud," Miss Southern Tier Dairy Queen whispers to Miss Mint Julep. "Wouldn't toss him off the porch for eating potato chips."

"Shhh," Miss Julep says, giggling, nodding toward me. "That's Willa's father."

We process in to a song by Kenny Rogers. Simon's "hero," Suzanna explained. Poor Tina and Ruby were so disappointed when they crashed the rehearsal dinner last night. The ushers were not the hunks they had imagined. Simon may be gorgeous, but his friends, most of them roadies for the band, look like they could use (a) a wardrobe makeover, (b) an exercise gym, (c) a haircut, and (d) a shower, not necessarily in that order. But when Tina and Ruby caught sight of Simon's little brother, Jace, "rhymes with 'face,'" standing there in his faded jeans, T-shirt, and cowboy hat, they started drooling like toddlers in front of the Swedish fish bin at Nana's candy store.

"He's the *best man*?" Tina said. "Oh, my God, Willa, that means he's *yours*."

"What?" I said.

"You're the maid of honor, silly. He's the best man. That makes him yours!"

When they took Jace's picture for the fourth time, I had to boot Tina and Ruby out the door.

Jace sat with me at the rehearsal dinner. He talked about football and rodeos, neither of which I know the slightest thing about, but I would have been speechless anyway. Jace is eighteen, going to college in the fall. "We've got an easy job tomorrow," he said. "Sixteen couples to follow walking in. How can we screw that up, right? I hand Simon the rings. You take Suzy's bouquet. 'I do,' 'I do,' we're done, let's party."

The sixteen bridesmaids process forward, and now it's our turn. Jace, "rhymes with 'face,'"— handsome, rugged cowboy face—holds out his arm to me and smiles in a way that gives me goose bumps even though it must be eighty degrees. "Ready?" he says.

"Yes."

I smell his cologne, feel the strong muscles of his arm as he draws me close beside him and leads us forward. I look up at him and he winks, and I think about the slow dance we will do at the reception.

When the sixteen bridesmaids and sixteen ushers, the maid of honor and hunky best man, are assembled at the edge of the pond, the two "ganolas" set forth. They move toward the floating dock and the white boat waiting in the center. When they arrive at the dock, the bride and groom disembark and join hands.

Simon helps Suzanna into the white boat, and together they row toward us.

It is a beautiful, simple gesture, the two of them rowing together. Not what you might have expected from a beauty queen. But then, Suzanna is so much more than that.

"Two people in a marriage have to row together," Suzanna explained to me. "That's what my mama taught me. That's what my mama's mama taught her. You come from different shores. You meet in the center. And then you row together."

After the ceremony the photographer takes countless pictures. The bridal party has a private champagne toast, and then, when the guests are all seated at the tables under the lemon yellow tents, the bandleader begins announcing the bridesmaids and ushers.

"And now, ladies and gentlemen, a special round of applause for the maid of honor, the bride's good friend, Miss Willa Havisham, escorted by the best man, brother of the groom, Mr. Jacey Finch."

Jace takes my arm, and we stroll in to the sound of clapping and whooping calls, and then the bride and groom dance their first dance, Elvis Presley's "Unchained Melody," and then the bridal party joins them.

Jace smiles at me and winks. He has the longest eyelashes I have ever seen. He wraps me like a hug in his arms. My cheek rests on the slope of his chest. My heart is drumming. I am slow-dancing with a beautiful cowboy. He is a great dancer. We move in perfect rhythm, no awkwardness at all. The sweet smell of his boutonniere mingles with the wilder scent of his cologne, and I feel like I am floating. The bandleader invites the rest of the guests to join in the dance. *Good, keep the music going.* My head is spinning. Jace leans his face down, rests his cheek in my hair. "Nice," he says. I close my eyes.

When I open them, I see JFK.

He's standing by the edge of the tent staring at me. Then he turns quickly, nearly knocking a lady over as he leaves.

"Joseph, wait." I head toward him, my heart pounding. I look for him. I search for him everywhere, but it's crowded, and then Suzy-Jube is hugging me, all happy. "Everything is perfect," she says. "Just the way I dreamed." And then I get swept up in the excitement of the wedding.

I'll call JFK tomorrow.

Everything was perfect, the food, the music . . . and the cake . . . the Bramblebriar signature wedding cake was the hit of the party. "It's delicious, just delicious," people said. Some asked for seconds. Mama Blazer had thirds. In fact, so many guests raved about the cake that Mom sent a waitress into the kitchen to get Rosie.

She came out shyly, wiping her hands on her apron. I motioned for her to come forward. I took the microphone from the emcee. "Ladies and gentlemen, I'd like to introduce my friend Ms. Rosalita Torres, the finest baker in Bramble."

People clapped, and Rosie nodded her head, pleased but modest.

And then all of a sudden Mama Blazer came rushing up like a cyclone, a bit tipsy from all the champagne, I think, and hugged Rosie so hard she nearly knocked her over, golden boa feathers flying everywhere. "Rosie, sugar," Mama B.

gushed. "You've got talent, honey. That's the best cake I've ever tasted, and believe me, I know cakes. Give me your phone number, honey. Papa B. and I are going to make you famous!"

CHAPTER 24

Two Stars Crossing

Don't know when I've seen such a lovely wedding. But I always cry. Don't know why it is, but I always cry. I just like to see young people happy, don't you? Oh, I think it's lovely.

—*Our Town*

"Thank you, thank you, thank you," Suzanna says, hugging me, then Mom, then me again as the last of the guests head off to bed. "Thank you, Stella, thank you, Willa. It was all that I dreamed of and more. And I *loved* the wishing well full of charms, Willa, and the dancing. . . ." She leans down to unstrap a glittery sandal. "My feet still think they're dancing. . . ."

Miss Shirley Happyfeet from Truro outdid herself again. She had Mama and Papa B. leading a conga line, and then she choreographed the sixteen bridesmaids in a "clam cakes number," sort of a high-stepping, leg-flashing Cape Cod version of the Rockettes, that had every guy in the place going wild.

The Bramblebriar signature wedding cake and the silver charms were the talk of the evening. "The wishing well was your idea?" Mom said. "How creative."

But even though it should have been one of the happiest nights of my life, I kept seeing JFK's face in my mind. Then one of the bridesmaids would pull me back on to the dance floor and Jace would swing me in his arms and I'd start having a good time again, and then a minute later my stomach would clench remembering JFK.

I just need to talk to him, to explain that the maid of honor and best man are *required* to dance together. It's just a custom, that's all. It's way too late to call his house. Maybe I'll write him a letter, then in the morning I'll bike over and tape it to his front door so he'll get it first thing.

Dear Joseph,
Why did you run off from the wedding so quickly? I was just dancing, that's all. He was the

best man and I was the maid of honor. We had
to dance together. It's a wedding tradition. Please
don't be mad. I'll see you at Mum's wedding,
okay?
Willa

I change into pajamas, snuggle into bed, but
cannot fall asleep. So many thoughts swirling
inside. Why did JFK have to get so mad? Couldn't
he at least have stayed for a minute so we could
talk? But I was dancing sort of close to Jace. I can
see why JFK would be angry. How would I feel if I
saw him dancing with Mariel?

I pull on a sweatshirt and head to Sam's office.
I climb up the narrow flight of stairs, push open
the door, and step out onto the widow's walk.

Ahhhh . . . cool, fresh air hits my face. The sky
is jet black and speckled with stars. Bramble stars.
I close my eyes, breathe in and out, feel the soft,
breeze on my cheeks. I take a deep breath and let
it go. It is so quiet and peaceful up here.

When I open my eyes, I see a *flash* in the sky,
one star burning brighter than the rest. Then all of
a sudden the star bursts and shoots downward.

And then *another flash*, a second star glowing brighter, brighter, and then it, too, begins to fall. I've never seen a shooting star before, now twice in one . . . The trail of the second star crosses the path of the first. They make an X in the sky.

I start to cry. It's so beautiful.

A sign, but what does it mean?

I'm wide awake now, so I head down to the kitchen to put the twelve charms in Mum and Riley's wedding cake. It's only my second wedding, but I have a feeling this will become one of our Bramblebriar traditions.

People had such fun with the charms at Suzanna's wedding, saying how something might be a good sign of this or that.

I know Mum will like the idea. She's forever saying signs are all around us. Beautiful surprises at every turn. If we look for them with an open heart.

Back in bed, I lie awake thinking about today, the expression on JFK's face—was he angry or jealous? I can't wait to drop off the note and talk to him tomorrow.

We invited everyone from Bramble United Community to join us here at the inn tomorrow after Mum and Riley's wedding. The Blazers will have left by then to set sail on the *Cape Queen*.

Mum told me she just wanted a simple brunch, but I knew she was concerned about costs. Mom and Sam and I decided that the reception would be our treat.

Mum will be so surprised. I can't believe she's getting married tomorrow. I can't believe she's leaving Bramble. . . .

I start to cry again. This time for a different reason. Why is everything so complicated all of a sudden? Just this spring life was so perfect, and now this summer it's all crazy. I hug my fluffy old one-eared koala bear, soft against my cheek.

Just before I fall asleep, I see the two stars kissing on the clear black slate of my mind. *X* marks the spot. A sign maybe.

But is it good or bad?

CHAPTER 25

Mum's Wedding Present

Now there are some things we all know, but we don't take'm out and look at'm very often. We all know that something is eternal. And it ain't houses and it ain't names, and it ain't earth, and it ain't even the stars . . . everybody knows in their bones that something is eternal, and that something has to do with human beings. All the greatest people ever lived have been telling us that for five thousand years and yet you'd be surprised how people are always losing hold of it. There's something way down deep that's eternal about every human being.

—*Our Town*

I wake up to the smell of coffee and the sound of rain rapping on the roof.

I forgot to hang the rosaries.

I look at the clock and leap out of bed. Mum's wedding is in two hours.

There's a knock on my door. "Come in, come in," I shout, moving around, still half asleep, trying to decide whether to shower first or go down and eat breakfast first or . . .

Rosie is holding a wooden tray. "Thought this would save you some time," she says. Warm blueberry muffins, juice, and coffee. Rosie smiles and shakes her head. "I don't know how you're doing it all, Willa. Two weddings back-to-back, and the maid of honor at both."

I take the tray and set it on my bed. "You are so sweet, Rosie, thank you." I give her a hug. "Are you managing the kitchen alone this morning?"

"No," Rosie says. "Daryl and Maggie are here."

"Your cake was such a hit yesterday, Rosie. You'll have to tell me the recipe."

"I don't know about that," Rosie says with a smile. "Your friend Mrs. Blazer said to keep it a secret. A tip-top secret. 'Don't even write it down,' she said."

"Oh, no." I see the note I was going to drop off at JFK's.

"What, Willa? What's wrong?"

I tell Rosie what happened last night.

"Give it to me," Rosie says. "The girls can handle the kitchen. What's his address? I need some fresh air anyway. Your friend Mrs. Blazer has my head swimming with all of her plans and ideas."

My dress for Mum's wedding is pale pink, a simple but elegant linen. I have blisters from yesterday's high heels. My feet sing *Thank you* when I slip on sandals.

I pick up the silver locket from my dresser. *Should I wear it or not?* And then I think, of course, if ever there was a day to celebrate two halves of a heart locking together as one, today is the day. And JFK will be there. Hopefully he's reading my note right now, realizing how he overreacted.

Every pew in BUC is packed. People are standing all around the perimeter, spilling out into the gathering space and out the front door, in the rain, with umbrellas.

I keep looking for JFK. I don't see him anywhere.

Riley's cousin Birch, the only relative Riley

keeps in touch with, took buses all the way from Alabama to be the best man. Birch is older than Riley. He has darker skin, a salt-and-pepper speckled beard. Like Riley, he moves slowly, deliberately, shoulders hunched like they've carried a ton of weight in his lifetime. When Birch laughs—which, like Riley, is quite often—his eyes laugh too.

"Miss Willa," he says, nodding at me at the back of the church. He crooks his crisp, tuxedoed arm upward, and I wrap my hand around it.

As we walk up the center aisle of BUC, this place I love so much, tears begin to well in my eyes. I am so happy for Mum and so very sad that she's leaving.

When Birch and I reach the front, we part and take our respective positions. The music stops and everyone stands. Up in the choir loft Mrs. Bellimo, in a stunning red hat with real roses around the brim, starts to play the organ. I know all the songs at BUC, we do a lot of singing every Sunday, but this is a melody I've never heard before. It has a soulful sound, like humming, rising up from someplace deep.

Mum and Riley process down the aisle together. Mum in the beautiful white satin and lace-trimmed gown we shopped for in Mashpee together. Riley in a white tuxedo with a rainbow-colored cummerbund and matching rainbow tie. I smile knowing he chose them to match Mum's multicolored minister's robe.

But today Mum isn't a minister. Today Mum is a bride. Today she's wearing a wedding dress, marrying the love of her life.

I scan the aisles for JFK. I don't see him anywhere.

When the ceremony is over and Mrs. Bellimo booms out the wedding march, there is not a dry eye in the place as Mum and Riley process out, smiling and glowing and laughing and waving, the happiest day of their lives.

Birch and I join the bride and groom for some photographs at the altar, and then we go outside with the others. Mom hands me one of the tiny vials filled with birdseed we planned to shower the lovebirds with.

Finally the rain has stopped and the sun is showing who's boss again.

Mum and Riley appear in the doorway, and a swell of cheering rises up. *"Congratulations!"* we shout, and toss the seeds, clapping, whistling, cameras flashing, all eyes on the happy couple.

Riley looks past us, his chin tilted up toward the sky. He smiles and points to something. "See that, Sully? God sent you a present."

We all turn to look.

A rainbow painted perfectly on that shimmering blue Cape Cod sky.

CHAPTER 26

I've Lost Him

EMILY: *Well, if you love me, help me. All I want is someone to love me.*
GEORGE: *I will, Emily.*

—*Our Town*

JFK never came to Riley and Mum's wedding.

I checked with Rosie, and she said she handed him the note herself.

"He probably had a game today, Willa," my mother said.

"That's right," Sam said. "It must be getting near play-offs."

Surely he'll come to Mum and Riley's surprise party at the inn. He promised he'd come when I told him about it. Everyone is here. So many people love Mum.

Mum laughs when she sees the bride and

groom figures on the top of her wedding cake. "Who's that skinny girl?" she says.

Lots of my friends from school are here. Alexa and Gus, Tina and Jessie, Ruby and Chris, Luke, Shefali, Trish, and Caroline.

Mum and Riley have a blast dancing with us. They could teach Miss Happyfeet some moves.

Tina keeps staring at me with a strange expression on her face. Through the toasts and testimonials and the "R-E-S-P-E-C-T" Aretha Franklin girls-only dance with Mum and Mom, Nana, Mrs. Bellimo, Mrs. Saperstone, Mrs. Sivler, Mrs. Belle—all the ladies of Bramble—I can tell Tina has something important to tell me. It's one of those things best friends know. We pick it up like radar.

"Tina, what's the matter?"

"Nothing," she says.

I try again later. "I know you want to tell me something, Tina, come on . . . *what?*"

"Nothing," she says.

I know she's lying. Now she's got me worried.

Finally, when Mum and Riley say good-bye and the last guests are leaving, Tina grabs my arm and says, "Okay, I can tell you now. I didn't want to say anything before because I didn't want to spoil . . ."

When she says the word "spoil," I know it's something about JFK. Something bad. "What, Tina? Just say it."

"Are you sure you want to know?"

"Yes. What?"

"Okay, well, Jessie and I were out on a date last night."

Last night. Suzanna and Simon's wedding reception.

"We were walking on the beach, and I happened to look up at the ledge by Clover Lane, and I saw this couple . . . sitting together . . . real close." Tina stares at me.

My stomach clenches.

"I'm pretty sure they were kissing," Tina says. "And then just as we passed by, the boy's head turned and . . . I'm so sorry, honey. . . ." Tina's face scrunches up, all sad. "But it was Joey . . . and the girl . . . the girl was Mariel Sanchez."

"*No,*" I say, slumping on to a chair. I feel dizzy, like I might faint. "It's all my fault, Tina. Joseph saw me slow-dancing with Jace Finch at the—"

"*Your fault?*" Tina jumps to my defense. "No way is it your fault, Willa. You didn't do anything wrong. *She's* the one. Where does that little witch live, anyway? I'll teach her to steal my best friend's boy. . . ."

Tina means well, but she's just making things worse. As soon as she leaves, I run upstairs, lock my door, and sob into my pillow so Mom and Sam won't hear.

I've lost him, I've lost him, I've lost him.

CHAPTER 27

Just Follow the Sunny Road

*The morning star always gets wonderful bright
the minute before it has to go,—doesn't it?*

—*Our Town*

When I wake up the next morning, my eyes are
red and swollen. I have no appetite for breakfast.
"Are you ready to go?" Sam asks in a gentle voice.
He doesn't press me for details.

We stop at Delilah's Florist to pick up my special order.

"Good thing your dad's here to help carry
these," Delilah says. "Six dozen, you said, Willa,
right?"

"Mum will love these," Sam says.

We meet Riley and the rental truck at the school

gym. I oversee the loading of the books. The boxes and boxes of Bramble books. There is a reporter and a photographer from the *Cape Cod Times* to cover the story. The books fill the entire truck.

"Good thing my new bride travels light," Riley says, laughing.

Sam and I follow Riley to Mum's place. Soon a new minister will be moving in.

I remember Mum's face lighting up when she talked about finally having a house of her own. "The church administration provides housing, but housing's not the same as a house," she said.

I have a fleeting thought about Come Home Cape Cod again. Rosie and Liliana could sure use a house. Mariel and her family need one even more, all of them cramped in that depressing old motel room. *What's wrong with you, Willa? Who cares about Mariel? That girl just stole your boyfriend. . . .*

When I see Mum sitting there waiting for us on her porch, I fight back an ocean of tears. *Be brave, Willa, be brave.* I picture all the times we sat on those steps talking about anything, everything, laughing over the littlest things, crying over the big stuff.

Inside I'm shouting, *Don't go, Mum, don't go*. Outside I put on a smiley face.

Riley and Sam load Mum's few bags and boxes into the back of the truck. Sam closes the doors, latches them.

"Those books will be so appreciated," Mum says. "I'll ask my friend to send pictures when the new school library is all set up."

Mum looks so happy, so excited about finally heading south, going home.

"You and your friends did another wonderful thing, Willa," she says. "Saving one library, starting another. I'm mighty proud of you, little sister."

I catch the cry in my throat. I suck the tears like soda through a straw, down, down into my chest, and lock them up tight for now.

This is Mum's time. Mum's time to be happy. I won't let her worry about me.

Sam and I tie a string of cans on the bumper. We tape on the JUST MARRIED banner Mom helped me make. She wanted to be here this morning too, but she wasn't feeling well. I wondered briefly if it was morning sickness.

"No good-byes, my Willa-like-a-willow-tree," Mum says, her big, beautiful brown eyes brimming with tears. She wipes her face and laughs. "All right, that's enough. If all these tears let loose, I'll make a whole new Atlantic right here on Main Street."

I laugh and then stop. I do my best to smile. I purse my lips together tight, making little squeaking sounds, pushing the sobs back down my throat.

They get in the van. Riley starts the engine. Mum pulls the seat belt across her chest.

Sam touches my shoulder. "Don't forget your gift," he whispers.

"These are for you, Mum." I hand her a bouquet of sunflowers, and then another, and another, and another and another, until the whole front seat is filled with happy, sunny yellow faces.

Two other faces look out at me.

Riley smiles and winks at me, then raises his chin and looks straight ahead.

"Oh, Willa . . ." Mum's voice cracks. She doesn't say anything for a few moments. "You are the child . . . the daughter I never had."

Mum looks at me with so much love, like she's making a mental photograph of me, every surface of her face quivering, moving, like the sea.

"I'll tell you what I'm going to do," Mum says, sniffing. She hitches herself up higher in the seat, a smile springing out on her face.

"I'm going to toss one of these sunflowers out the window every hundred miles or so, in every state we go through. I'm going to plant seeds all the way South, so when you come to visit . . . soon, I hope . . . you'll know right where to find me. Okay, honey? Just follow the sunny road."

"Okay, Mum." I smile my all-time bravest smile.

Then they pull away, waving, horn beep-beeping.

Sam puts his arm around me, safe and solid like a harbor.

At the corner the truck slows down.

Mum tosses out the first flower.

She leans out the window and waves.

She waves and waves, and I wave too, until we can't see each other anymore.

Then Sam hugs me and I start to sob. Sam is crying too.

Sulamina Mum was the sun in Bramble.

It won't ever be as bright without her.

CHAPTER 28

Father's Day

GEORGE: *Oh . . . I don't think it's possible to be perfect, Emily.*
EMILY: *Well, my father is, and as far as I can see your father is.*
There's no reason on earth why you shouldn't be, too.

—*Our Town*

When Sam and I get home, Nana meets us at the front door. "Stella needs you upstairs," she says to Sam.

I can tell something is very wrong.

"Let's go out on the porch," Nana says softly to me.

She sits on the wicker couch. I sit beside her. One of the guests, a nice woman, a teacher from Rochester, New York, walks toward us like she wants to chat, but then she sees the look on

Nana's face and sets off down the stairs.

"Honey, I'm sorry," Nana says, reaching out to put her hand over mine. "I have some sad news. Your mother lost the baby this morning."

Lost the baby. I always think that is such a stupid thing to say. *Lost the baby.* Well, where did you lose it? The supermarket? The post office? The dentist's office? *Where?*

"No," I say.

"I'm so sorry, Willa. I know it's a shock."

"No," I say.

Nana shakes her head sadly. "The chance of miscarriage is greater when a woman is Stella's age and . . ."

Miss carriage. The carriage is missing. Well, where could it be? I feel so angry I want to explode.

"You didn't blame her, did you, Nana?" I stand up, my body shaking. "You didn't say she should have slowed down or eaten more meat or—"

"Willa." Nana sounds shocked. Then she reaches up and gently touches my face.

"Oh, Nana, I'm sorry," I fall back down beside her, crying.

She smooths my hair, rocks me back and forth. "It's all right, honey. I know, I know. . . ."

***

Sam takes Mom to the hospital for a surgical procedure. When they come home, she is groggy and crying.

"Let's just let her sleep," Sam says.

In the morning I bring her a cup of tea. "Willa," she says, propping herself up, smiling bravely, but then she starts crying.

"It's okay, Mom. It's okay." I hug her and smooth her hair.

At school Tina is so kind to me. All my friends are. JFK says he's sorry, but he doesn't hug me. I can't worry about him right now. My mom, my family, needs me.

Sunday is Father's Day. Mom is still in bed.

"It was such a blow," Nana says when she comes to drop off a casserole. Friends and neighbors keep bringing us food. I guess that's what people do when something sad happens. They bring food.

"She was so happy, and then so sad," Nana says. "Give her time, honey. There are many hard things to face in this world, but few harder than the loss of a baby."

And I was going to be a big sister.

Father's Day.

I looked forward to this day for so long. I planned to say that word, "Dad," to Sam, but now I can't. It would be too sad for him. For three whole months Sam thought he was going to be a new dad, a new father to a sweet, tiny baby, maybe even a boy.

I see Sam out working in the garden.

I want to talk to him.

I see Sam heading to the kitchen to start preparing dinner.

I want to talk to him.

It's late and the last guest has finished playing a favorite song on the piano. A breeze is lifting the curtains, better to hear the crickets chirping.

Go, Willa, the voice inside me says. *Go, now.*

Sam is sitting in the library, his head nodding forward into a book.

"Sam?"

He sees me and smiles. "Willa."

He isn't annoyed that I've disturbed him, caught him nearly falling asleep.

I walk to his chair. I stare steel-straight into his eyes. Blue to blue.

"Happy Father's Day . . . *Dad.*"

Sam's lips quiver.

"Thank you, Willa. You don't know what a gift . . ."

"I can't imagine how sad you must be losing the baby," I say. "I know how much you and Mom wanted . . . I did too . . . and I know it's not nearly the same. . . ."

"Willa," he says. He shakes his head. "It is so hard to lose the baby. But the gift you are giving me . . ." He sucks in a deep breath and smiles his beautiful, wonderful special Sam smile.

"We chose to have a baby. But *you*, you *chose me* to be your dad. And I am deeply honored."

CHAPTER 29

Opening Night

Look, it's clearing up. The stars are coming out.

—*Our Town*

It's June 21. Opening night for *Our Town*.

JFK and I finally had a chance to talk after practice the other day. I explained about how I was just dancing with Jace, and he said, "Don't worry about it," but I could tell he was still mad.

"Give him some time to cool off," Tina said. "Boys have big egos. Give him some space. He'll come around."

How much space does he need? I can't stand us not talking to each other.

Every night at practice as I heard him say "I love you, Emily," staring into Mariel's eyes, every time I watched them kiss in the wedding scene, I felt my stomach being wrung out like a towel, *twisted, twisted, twisted,* until every last drop dripped out.

The director finally told us her name after our final rehearsal last night.

Abilene Muhlfelder.

"Why didn't you tell us before?" I asked.

"Because it was irrelevant," she said. "In *Our Town*, I am the director. And you are the Stage Manager. And Mariel is Emily. Our other identities have no place in this theater hall. No place on this stage."

Opening night is sold out. I find a crack in the red velvet curtains and spot them there in the first row. My family. Mom and Dad and Nana.

Tina said she would be here. I'm sure she's out there somewhere. And Mrs. Saperstone, and all my friends. I feel Gramp here too. I picture Mum, then force myself to focus. On cue I walk out onto the stage. I feel the heat of the lights on my face.

I am not Willa. I am the Stage Manager. I take a deep breath and begin:

"'This play is called "Our Town." It was written by Thornton Wilder; produced and directed by Miss Abilene Muhlfelder. . . .'"

I finish my first lines, and other actors take the

stage, and as much as I try to stay in character, I can't help thinking, *You are JFK, not George; you are Mariel, not Emily.*

That night on the beach you said that when you kissed her in the wedding scene, you'd be acting, but when you kiss me, it's for real. . . .

And then it's act 2, the wedding scene, and Emily—Mariel—is processing in on Mr. Webb's arm, and she meets up with George—JFK—and they come to stand together in front of me. In this scene I play the minister. I have to marry them.

JFK and Mariel have their backs to the audience, facing me. I alone can see their eyes.

The rings are exchanged. He kisses her.

And then, for the briefest moment, JFK tilts his face ever so slightly toward me, and with the eye that only I can see—not Mariel—not the audience — JFK winks at me.

On the outside I retain the composure of the Stage Manager.

Inside, Willa and the entire towns of butterflies are doing a happy dance.

CHAPTER 30

A Welcome Wash-Ashore

This town's gettin' bigger every year.

—*Our Town*

The curtain closes on opening night to thunderous applause. The actors with the smaller roles walk back out on stage first, and then the Gibbs family, the Webb family, JFK, then Mariel, then me. I hear Mom and Nana shouting, "Bravo, bravo." Sam whistling. Tina cheering like she's at a Patriots game, *"Go, Willa! Go, Willa!"*

Backstage, Mom hands me a bouquet of yellow roses. Sam takes pictures. I see Mariel Sanchez's father, his face brimming with pride, shaking his clenched fists victoriously in the air. Mariel is being interviewed by the arts and entertainment reporter for the *Cape Cod Times*. The photographer checks the spelling of her name for the caption.

Mariel was the perfect Emily. Too bad her mother wasn't here.

I am dying to talk to JFK, but it will have to wait until after the cast party.

Abilene Muhlfelder shakes my hand. "Well done," she whispers.

JFK's father, Mr. Kennelly, walks toward me with a woman I have never seen before. "Willa, if you have a minute, I'd like to introduce you to Mrs. Emma Barrett."

The pretty woman, silver white hair, pale blue gray eyes with specks of amber, maybe Nana's age, extends her hand. "It is so nice to finally meet you, Willa," she says.

Behind us, Mariel and her father are leaving. I don't see JFK anywhere.

"I've just moved into New Seabury," Mrs. Barrett says. "My husband and I recently retired. We've always wanted to live on Cape Cod. It's been our dream for so many. . ."

I'm trying to focus on this nice lady, but I want to go find JFK, *now*.

". . . and we've been subscribing to the *Cape Cod Times*," she continues, "trying to learn as much as we can, in anticipation of becoming 'good wash-ashores,' as they say. We know that transplants aren't always welcomed with open arms. . . ."

Mr. Kennelly laughs. "You are the most welcome sort of wash-ashore, Emma."

Mrs. Barrett smiles. "Well, thank you, Stephen. We will certainly try to—"

"Excuse me," I say, flustered and trapped. "But I need to go. It was nice meeting you, Mrs. Barrett. Welcome to Cape Cod."

"Wait a second, Willa," Mr. Kennelly says.

"Yes, just one moment, please," Mrs. Barrett says. "I wanted to tell you, Willa, that my husband and I followed the story of your saving the Bramble Library. That was wonderful. And then more recently we read your editorial letter urging people to help support the work of the new Come Home Cape Cod organization, and well, we thought, good for her. Look at how one girl is making such a difference."

This is lovely, but I really need to find my boyfriend.

"Life has been good to me and Jonathan. It's time we gave something back."

Good, good, good, but I really need to go . . .

"And so, in celebration of our fiftieth wedding anniversary, we have decided to put a half a million dollars into an endowed trust fund, from which Come Home Cape Cod will be able to draw money to build one new house a year for a deserving Cape Cod family. And I just wanted to personally thank you for inspiring us."

"Aaaah," I gasp, speechless.

I feel a hand on one shoulder and then on the other. Mom and Dad are behind me, eyes bright with pride. They heard the whole thing.

And so did JFK.

He is standing behind my parents with a smile on his beautiful face. He winks at me and nods toward the door like, *Come on, let's get out of here.*

"Are you sure I'm still good enough for you?" JFK says. "When word gets out about this, television crews will be descending on Bramble and thousands of guys all over the country will see you on the morning news, see how pretty you are. . . ."

Pretty . . . I like that. That's light-years better than

cute. But what about Mariel? And so I just blurt it out.

"Tina saw you and Mariel together on the beach the night of Suzanna's wedding."

"*What?* You mean the night you were dancing all hot and heavy with the cowboy?"

"He was the best man, Joseph. It's a tradition. The maid of honor and best man have to dance—"

"Well, you didn't have to enjoy it so much."

"At least I didn't *kiss* him. Tina saw you kissing Mari—"

"Tina's wrong," JFK says, angry. "Tell Tina to mind her own business."

"Well, what were you doing with Mariel, then?"

"I was being a friend," he says. He stands up, angry, walks away a bit, turns around. "Mare was upset that night. I felt really bad for her. She had sent her mother a letter asking her to come home for opening night, telling her that she was going to play Emily in *Our Town*, just like she did. Her mother never responded. Mare's letter got returned, no forwarding address. I was just being a friend, Willa. That's all."

CHAPTER 31

A New Day

I always say: happiness, *that's the great thing!
The important thing is to be happy.*

—*Our Town*

My alarm goes off. I look at the clock. If I hurry,
I can make it.

When I get to the beach, there is already someone sitting on the top step of the beach stairs by
the wild pink rugosa bushes. My spot.

Mariel smiles when she sees me.

"Good morning," she says.

"Good morning."

Mariel slides across the step, making room for
me.

I sit down.

We stare out at the horizon.

It's the end of June. School's out.

Two whole long, glorious months stretching out like forever before me.

Later I'll take my summer reading list to Sweet Bramble Books, grab a bag of taffy, then pack a lunch, head to the beach, and read all afternoon. I'll bring my journal too. So many memories I want to capture before I forget.

JFK's team is out on the Vineyard. Tina's off on a shopping spree with her mother.

Maybe I'll ask Mariel to join me.

I made a promise to Mum to be nice to her, and besides, I think we could be good friends. We have a lot in common. Maybe even more than Tina and I do.

So much has happened in the few short months since I first saw Mariel standing on the jetty. I was so angry at this mysterious girl for disrupting my perfect little world. My beach. My boyfriend. My library. My town.

Today we sit silently, lost in our thoughts, waiting for the same sun.

A red ribbon tops the orange one now. It is almost time.

Our Town was a good experience, but I don't think acting is my talent. The reviewer said I gave "a solid if uninspired performance" as the Stage Manager, but that a Bramble newcomer, Miss Mariel Sanchez, was "brilliant in the role of Emily." She "lit up the stage" and "conveyed an emotional depth truly stunning in one so young." The headline read, A STAR IS BORN IN BRAMBLE.

And yet, surprisingly, I am not jealous. Mariel has her gifts and I have mine.

Maybe I'm meant to write the plays, and Mariel to perform them.

"Should be soon," I say.

"Yes."

We sit, side by side, waiting.

Mariel has as much right to be here as I do.

Bramble is her town too.

There is plenty of beach for both of us. Plenty of boys. Plenty of books.

I close my eyes and smile. I can picture it all by heart.

"Here it comes," she says.

And then, there it is.

A new dawn.

A new day.

Thank you.

"Willa's Pix 3"

Recommended by Willa Havisham

A Gift from the Sea, Anne Morrow Lindbergh
Jane Eyre, Charlotte Brontë
Leaves of Grass, Walt Whitman
My Ántonia, Willa Cather
Our Town, Thornton Wilder
Rebecca, Daphne du Maurier
The Scarlet Letter, Nathaniel Hawthorne
Their Eyes Were Watching God, Zora
    Neale Hurston
To Kill a Mockingbird, Harper Lee
Walden, Henry David Thoreau
The Wonderful Wizard of Oz, L. Frank Baum
Wuthering Heights, Emily Brontë

Acknowledgments

Since my first book, *How Prudence Proovit Proved the Truth About Fairy Tales,* was published in the summer of 2004, followed that fall by *26 Big Things Small Hands Do,* and that spring by my first novel, *The Wedding Planner's Daughter*, and during the writing of the next five books, *The Cupid Chronicles; Mack McGinn's Big Win; Kip Campbell, The Funeral Director's Son; Catching the Sun;* and now *Willa by Heart,* I have been honored to visit with many schools, libraries, bookstores, reading councils, and other organizations where it has been a *joy* to talk about reading and writing and books, books, books.

Each experience has inspired me to dig deeper, and I am profoundly grateful for the questions, comments, and kindness of countless people: teachers, librarians, booksellers, parents, principals, and, most of all, the young readers who share their wisdom, energy, and enthusiasm, like fireflies, like sunflowers, like shooting stars.

And so, in the order of when we first "book-talked" together, I wish to thank my friends at: Guilderland Elementary School; Duanesburg Elementary School; C. V. Starr Intermediate; Tamarac Middle School; the Book House at Stuyvesant Plaza; Barnes and Noble, Colonie, New York; Barnes and Noble, Saratoga Springs, New York; the Open Door Bookstore; Troy Public Library; Eight Cousins Bookstore; Market Street Bookshop; Blackwood & Brouwer; the Bookmark; New England Bookseller's Association; Barnes and Noble, Niskayuna, New York; Children's Literature Connection Fall Festival of Books, Emma Willard School; North Atlantic Independent Booksellers Association; Russell Sage College; Borders, Colonie, New York; Borders, Saratoga Springs, New York; Christ the King toddler playgroup; the Victorian Ball, benefiting the Troy Public Library; Green Chimneys; American Library Association; Elsmere Elementary School; Boght Hills Elementary School; Montgomery Fulton Reading Council; Thomas O'Brien Academy of Arts and Sciences; Schoharie Reading Council; School 14, Troy, New York; the College of Saint Rose; Susan Odell Taylor School; SCBWI, Eastern Pennsylvania Poconos Retreat; the

Academy of the Holy Names; "Got Books, Let's Read II," Hodge-Podge Conference; the Ark Community Charter School; Marston Mills Library; Market Block Books; Guilderland Public Library; Bethlehem Public Library; Rutger's Council on Children's Literature; School 18, Troy, New York; Southgate Elementary School; Mother-Daughter Book Club at Jefferson Elementary School; Market Block Books; Hamagrael Elementary School; Capital Area School Development Association; The Doane Stuart School; Sullivan Reading Council; Lynwood Elementary School; Watervliet Elementary School; Green Meadow Elementary School; Elmer Avenue School; Greenfield Elementary School; Mother-Daughter Book Club, Newburgh Free Library; Clifton-Park-Halfmoon Public Library; John Evans Elementary School; New York State Reading Association; Mother-Daughter Book Club, Niskayuna, New York; Borders, Bridgewater, New Jersey; Red Fox Books; Bradt Elementary School; Poestenkill Elementary School; Glenmont Elementary School; Charlton Heights Elementary; Birchwood Elementary; Gloversville Middle School Authorfest; Westmere Elementary School;

Barnes and Noble, Saratoga; Dog Ate My Homework, Glens Falls, New York; Martin H. Glynn School; Genet Elementary School; Skribblers Magazine Awards; Albany Academy for Girls; Novello Reading Festival, Charlotte, North Carolina; and the Rochester Children's Book Festival.

When we meet again, I look forward to hearing what you are reading and writing these days!

Read on, write on, dream big.

Also, my very special thanks to Alyssa Eisner-Henkin; my editor, Emily Meehan, and Courtney Bongiolatti; my friend forever in spirit, Mary Beth Moore Barrett; my mother, Peg Spain Murtagh; my husband, Tony Paratore; and most especially, with love always, my three sons, my *suns*, my stars, Christopher, Connor, Dylan.

Shine on, shine on, shine on.

About the Author

Coleen Murtagh Paratore is the author of the acclaimed The Wedding Planner's Daughter series as well as *Mack McGinn's Big Win*. She makes her home in Albany, New York, and Mashpee, Massachusetts, with her husband and her three sons. She's also a believer in community theater, kismet, and Cape Cod.